ONLY THE RU' CAN PLAY

In the city of London, the *Career Development Functions* rooms are situated on the tenth floor of International Synthetics. There, people undergo the 'Fifth Executive Course'. The participants expect a gruelling challenge — one in which men fight for power — knowing that the going will be tough. But they don't expect one of their members to die in gruesome circumstances. So, is this a test of their reactions — or the insane ambitions of one of their own number?

JOHN BURKE

---◆---

ONLY THE RUTHLESS CAN PLAY

Complete and Unabridged

LINFORD
Leicester

First published in Great Britain

First Linford Edition
published 2012

British Library CIP Data

Burke, John Frederick, *1922* –
   Only the ruthless can play. - -
   (Linford mystery library)
   1. Detective and mystery stories.
   2. Large type books.
   I. Title II. Series
   823.9'14–dc23

   ISBN 978–1–4448–1292–3

Published by
F. A. Thorpe (Publishing)
Anstey, Leicestershire

Set by Words & Graphics Ltd.
Anstey, Leicestershire
Printed and bound in Great Britain by
T. J. International Ltd., Padstow, Cornwall

This book is printed on acid-free paper

For
JEAN
for more reasons
than I could list
on one page

1

Jessica awoke that morning to the usual pain of impending loss. It was not intense any longer — just nagging and inevitable. Andrew would be going away as he had so many times gone away. After two years of it she was able to cope. Perhaps, she sometimes thought, she wouldn't know what to do if it weren't there.

Andrew was already out of bed. She had been awakened by the familiar sensation of his sliding away. Reluctant to open her eyes, she was nevertheless conscious of the smooth way in which he managed it. He could draw up his feet and swing them out on to the floor without disturbing the bed-clothes. One might almost have imagined that he was being considerate, not wanting to wake one; yet this was something which never failed to wake her. She could sleep through a thunderstorm or the sudden bark of a sports car along Old Brompton

Road, but when Andrew slid silently away he dragged her up from sleep.

She turned over and opened her eyes.

His every movement and sequence of movements were always the same. That was what came of being an ambitious potential executive with time and motion study training. Never off duty, never forgetful. Don't walk twice across a room when once will do. Don't get bedclothes in a tangle and don't get paper tissues twisted when taking them from the box. When going into the bathroom turn on the hot tap while brushing your teeth so that the water will be hot by the time you are ready for it. Arrange clothes in the bedroom so that they can be stepped into in the right order. A glance at the wrist-watch to check the time. A flick of the comb through the hair before putting the jacket on: always before, never afterwards.

Jessica wondered if this was how his wife, too, saw him.

He adjusted the handkerchief in his top pocket.

She said: 'And your money.'

He smiled warily at her in the glass. 'Mm?'

'Your money,' she said. 'It goes in your right-hand pocket.'

'Of course.' He took up his loose change from the dressing table. He grew swiftly irritated if reminded of something which he had in fact not forgotten.

Jessica pushed herself up in bed. 'I'll get you something to eat before you go.'

'You'll do no such thing. I'll have a cup of coffee on the way in. Treat yourself to another ten minutes in bed.'

'It's no treat when I'm on my own.'

They had this same little discussion each time. She knew it was stupid and unreasonable of her but was driven to it. However often and however resolutely he moved away from her she tried despairingly to hold on to him.

She said: 'This evening . . . ?'

Andrew smiled again. Now it was a neat, careful smile. His lips, so demanding in the night, were now thin and reluctant. The divisions were all so tidy in his mind. There were things he did not wish her to say to him in the morning and

3

things he would not say to her. He did not like her to put her arms round him in the morning. He preferred her not to be naked in the morning.

He was looking at the door. Already he was far away — a tall man with brown, determined eyes, sandy hair that glinted grey above his ears, a blunt chin and large hands that were always competent and often brutal . . . a businessman, a stranger in her bedroom, trying to find a polite way of saying goodbye and getting out.

'This will be my last evening with Muriel,' he said patiently. 'I can't very well stay out. That would really cause trouble — now, wouldn't it?'

Jessica was all in favour of there being trouble. Not so long ago he had talked savagely of provoking just such trouble. She wanted to remind him that today was an anniversary, but he wouldn't have liked it. Two years ago today she had moved into this flat and two years ago today he had said that he would soon be leaving his wife and coming to live with her. No, he wouldn't have been pleased if she had reminded him of that.

He said: 'Well . . . '

'Well,' she said.

He picked up his brief-case and came towards the bed. He stooped and kissed her. She was determined to let him go in silence, but as he reached the door she heard herself saying: 'We'll be able to manage something while the Course is on. Nobody will notice.'

'Jess, we've already gone over this. It would be silly to sacrifice everything — '

'Everything?' His hoped-for promotion, his career, his reputation, the wife he said he detested . . . that was what he meant. She said: 'There's bound to be an opportunity. I know these Executive Courses. I ought to — I've shepherded the victims through enough of them in my time. There won't be any risk. In the hotel, or when we go up to the plant at Belby . . . '

'When the Course is ended,' he said heavily, 'I'll come round.'

'You make it sound like an arduous duty.'

'Jess, you know I want to be with you.'

Did she? Did he? It used to be once a

week. Then once a fortnight. Now there was no rhythm, no pattern: unlike everything else in his neatly calculated life, there was no set routine for this. She tried to tell herself it was better this way. She would probably not have wanted him to come home to her every night. She was growing accustomed to things as they were and wouldn't have wanted him to be there always. That was what she told herself.

'I really must get a move on,' said Andrew.

'I'll see you tomorrow.'

'Yes. But, Jess . . . ' He was quickly contriving the right blend of firmness, gentleness and faint reproach. 'You know what the results of this Course mean to me. This is the breakthrough — or failure. I can't afford to relax. I'm up against tough opposition. I can't let myself be distracted.'

'No,' she said. 'Of course not. I know.'

'There's my girl.'

He looked at his watch once more and turned away. Jessica rolled over on her side to watch him go. At the door he waved self-consciously as though from a train drawing away from a station platform. She waved back. After the door had closed she heard the rattle of the hanger as he took his overcoat out of the hall cupboard. Then there was the click of the front door.

She turned back towards the dressing-table mirror. He had gone. He had left her room and her mirror. It reflected a tilted pattern of wallpaper and a corner of the ceiling. A short time ago Andrew's face had been there. Now there was not even a lingering ghost.

From this angle she could not see herself in the glass. It didn't matter. She knew all that the mirror could tell her. She was Jessica Rogers, she was twenty-eight. She had fair hair and hazel eyes, her upper lip would be bruised because of Andrew last night, and there would be a red mark on her left shoulder. She had a flat of her own, a red Mini-Minor, and a view into a square that was really an oblong of yellowish grass shaded by sycamores and a lime tree. She had a job, a life of her own, and a lover.

Funny word, lover. It sounded odd, as any word does if you say it over a few times; particularly at this time of day. Perhaps Andrew was right: one ought to be prosaic in the morning.

Jessica forced herself to get out of bed and draw the curtains.

The April morning was still and opaque on the square. There was a faint haze which would remain a haze through most of the day, tinted by spring sunlight so that the houses opposite would glow through the trees in the afternoon. But she would not be here this afternoon. She would be making the last-minute arrangements for supplies of leather binders and pencils to members of the Intersyn Fifth Executive Course, and checking the list of names ready for tomorrow.

You know what the results of this Course mean to me . . . Oh, yes, she knew all right. Promotion for the star pupils. A job as General Manager in one of the overseas subsidiaries or top grade personnel work in the production plants. High level Public Relations and liaison posts. After they had watched you and questioned you and lured you on in question and answer, challenge and reaction, they would assess your potentialities as a manager, your ability to handle men and figures and campaigns and technicalities.

Success would also mean her seeing less of Andrew.

He had evaded this admission but she knew the score as well as he did. She had been Course Secretary for long enough to know that success wasn't something that you achieved once and for all. When you got to the top you had to work to stay there. You had to show that you were worthy of the Company's confidence in you. And the Company liked its top executives to be married and settled. It liked them to fit into its established scheme and to accept its established values. It wanted mature, responsible men. It didn't like them to visit younger unmarried female employees in South Kensington love nests.

Jessica began to dress. However much Andrew might say to her in the frenzied, ecstatic darkness, whatever promises he might give or imply, she knew he was unlikely to leave his wife if he came through this Course triumphant.

Muriel said: 'It's just another excuse. I've said so all along. You're looking forward to being away from me all that time.'

Andrew nudged his brief-case along the sofa and put his head back, closing his eyes for a few seconds. 'You know perfectly well what it means to us,' he said wearily. 'It shows I'm in the running for a top job. It's what I've worked for. It's one of the really big things. I haven't slogged away so hard all these years for nothing.'

'I'd sooner you stayed at home and gave some of your attention to me,' she pouted, 'and didn't try so hard.'

'Once you've started, you can't stop. You know that. God knows I've told you often enough.'

'God knows,' she agreed, 'you have.'

He banged his hand down against the edge of the new sofa. 'You don't object to the money. You use it up fast enough. You'll be glad of an increase when I get it.'

'I'd sooner see more of you than more money.'

It was simply not true. Even as a debating point it was feeble. But Muriel was shameless in her arguments, utterly convinced of the truth of whatever she was saying at the moment she said it.

Andrew said: 'What about a drink?'

For an instant there was a possibility that she might argue even on this. If he had phrased it carelessly — 'Couldn't we have a drink?' or 'For God's sake let's have a drink' — she would certainly have used it against him. But by lobbing it casually at her as though not worrying whether she caught it or not, he had given her no easy way of retaliating. Besides, she wanted a drink herself. It was not a truce but it was at least a lull. She poured a large whisky for each of them.

They drank. He ought to try some genuinely pleasant gambit, some jokingly affectionate remark that would make her smile and somehow open up the evening for them. But it wouldn't work. It had ceased to work a long time ago. All he could do was wait until she came gradually up to the boil again — up to what he thought of as her critical distillation point.

Muriel put her drink down. It had briefly soothed her and then provided new energy. She said:

'So I won't be hearing from you for heaven knows how many weeks?'

'The weeks,' he said, 'are fixed. I've given you all the details. I can see you the weekend before we go north to the plant. And no bar has been placed on our writing letters.'

'I know your letters,' she said. ' "Having wonderful time, glad you're not here." '

Her flaxen hair was as sleek and smooth as ever, but like her voice its brightness had hardened and taken on a brassy artificiality. The slightly irregular mouth that had once seemed mocking, knowledgeable and desirable was now permanently twisted so that it wrenched at her words as they came out and distorted them. He must have been very unobservant fifteen years ago not to have seen how she would shape up and how the amusing petulance would cease to be amusing. But he hadn't seen and now he had this on his hands. In his job it wouldn't have happened: he wouldn't have committed Intersyn to a lifetime programme on the basis of a fascinating new theory that might not work out in practice; no chemist's enthusiasm over an apparent revolution in polymerisation reactions would get him to recommend the buying in of new machinery and new moulds until the pilot plant had been driven to exhaustion under all stresses, all temperatures, all conditions. Unfortunately human beings could not be evaluated in quite the same way. Muriel had started out glossy, smooth-surfaced and beautiful. He had thought she would be malleable, but she had congealed too soon. Something had gone wrong and she had hardened instead of remaining pliable. He would never understand why. All he knew was that when a thing like this happened there was no way of going back and starting again: once the material was set, it was set. At this stage a sensible man abandoned the whole project and started again.

But the Company wouldn't like that.

He said: 'We get two weekends off during the Course. The one before we go north and one — '

'Decent of them. Like being in the Army, or at school.'

'If a man's not willing to give up six weeks in order to set himself up for life, the Company wouldn't be far wrong in thinking that he's not the sort of man they need for the really responsible jobs.'

'The Company,' she said on a dying fall of disparagement.

'When we met,' he reminded her, 'you were very impressed by my being there. You knew you were on to a good thing. So did your mother and father.'

'My father,' she said, 'never spent a day away from my mother during their whole married life.'

'Your father,' he said, 'never earned more than five hundred pounds a year and they lived in a Council house which you told me over and over again you hated like poison.'

'Oh, you talk such bloody nonsense,' she said.

He knew he had scored. When she said he was talking nonsense she was telling him that he spoke the clear, precise truth.

Now he could afford to be generous, knowing that patience and generosity made her angrier than anything else. He told her in a reasonable tone how the course was organised and how many other people would be on it and implicitly, complacently appealed to her to see his point of view and sit back and wait while he worked for their future — or, if she preferred, to go out and enjoy herself while he applied his whole mind to the task of coming out ahead of all the other contestants. For it was a contest. And many of his rivals would have a head start over him. They had been to the right schools, knew the right people; could even be related to directors or friends of directors.

'You're watched the whole time,' he said. 'When you're drinking in the bar they decide whether you're carrying it off with the right social grace. They like to know if you can argue a knotty problem without putting your opponent's back up.

15

And by the time you reach the special dinner at the end of the Course — '

'Wives invited?' asked Muriel harshly.

'I'm afraid not.'

'I'd always heard that big companies like to have wives along. It's got a lot to do with the man's career. They judge the wives as well.'

She picked up distorted fragments of so many things from so many sources; picked them up clumsily and applied them wrongly. In spite of himself he said: 'That would finish us, wouldn't it?'

Her face puckered with contrived misery. She had been more than half wanting him to say something like that so that she could wallow in the luxury of being wounded. It happened a dozen times a week and it bored and exasperated him at the same time, and also — as it was meant to do — filled him with feelings of guilt. She actively sought unhappiness and then turned it back upon him. She made him feel guilt where there was no logical reason for guilt.

He said: 'Look, Muriel, you know I didn't mean it.'

'I don't. I don't know any such thing.'

This showed every sign of being a wonderful evening, he thought bitterly. As a matter of principle he had to spend the final evening before the Course started with his wife, but he had known all along that it would be like this. She said she wanted to see more of him and wished he could spend more of his time with her; yet when he was here she used him only as a sounding board for her dissatisfactions. He would have been happier with Jess, having a quiet meal with Jess, going to bed with Jess.

It had to be admitted, though, that Jess too was getting querulous nowadays. Even in her company this evening there would have been resentful overtones. As if it weren't enough to feel irrationally guilty about Muriel, he felt twitches of guilt about Jess. Did one have to be plagued with guilt over every woman, every damned little thing?

The trouble is, he said to himself, that men have consciences; women only have emotions.

Resolutely he excluded the two women

from his mind. He and Muriel had dinner together and talked in bursts of rasping hostility, making no communication. Finally they went to bed together and he even made love to her — or, at any rate, went through the motions. She gave no sign of pleasure; but if he had left her alone and not touched her she would have said, 'Oh, so I don't appeal to you any more?' or something of that sort and they would have been awake half the night arguing. As it was, he had grown skilled at performing the routine while his attention remained uncommitted.

He wasn't going to be defeated by Muriel or by anyone. He had taught himself to survive. The more she nagged, the more he threw himself into his work. She had an abrasive effect on him that perhaps was no bad thing.

He clung to one certainty: whatever Muriel did or didn't do, whatever complaints she made, whatever she said or didn't say, he was going to come through this Course with flying colours. For the next six weeks he was going to be unflinchingly single-minded. Nothing must be allowed to stand in the way. To reach the top in Intersyn you had to be quite clear about your objective and quite ruthless.

He was sorry for anyone on the Course who was rash enough to challenge him.

2

The offices of International Synthetics had occupied two floors of a grimy building in High Holborn in the immediate post-war years. Within a very short time they spread out over half a new office block behind Cheapside. Intersyn then carried out one of the biggest industrial recruiting campaigns ever known, coaxing graduates into their production and marketing departments and forging links with foreign companies whose staff could contribute information and know-how to the central office. At a time when nearly every government in the world was introducing legislation to smash cartels and restrictive trading practices, Intersyn blandly formed new companies and bound them up in trading agreements which were legally unassailable but which depended more and more on a central guiding authority. Headquarters staff multiplied. A whole new building was needed. The Intersyn Tower rose above the glass and concrete blocks which had been dropped around the City of London like a giant's casually discarded toys.

Some architects and newspaper columnists called the tower a skinny monstrosity. Others waxed ecstatic about the slender upthrust which counterbalanced the squarer aspects of so many adjoining buildings, and referred to it as a twentieth-century substitute for a Wren spire. People who worked in it grumbled to one another about the faults in the central heating and air-conditioning systems, moaned about the sameness of the food in the canteen, and complained of suffering from claustrophobia, of being smothered, and of contracting skin troubles from the synthetic soap dispensers in the washrooms; but when talking to outsiders they became instinctively defensive and even enthusiastic about the smoothness of the organisation and the way in which everything had been thought of — everything for the comfort of staff from the cradle to the grave, everything that soothed petty irritations and enabled them to concentrate on their work.

Jessica approached the hard-edged tower along a segment of road that would not be finished off until the buildings on both sides were finished. The rawness of this road contrasted oddly with the gleaming, glassy suaveness of the Intersyn headquarters. Even after three years with the firm, taking the same route nearly every morning, she was conscious of the clash: it might almost have been deliberately arranged by Intersyn so that employees should feel the difference between the ragged outside world and the all-embracing efficiency of the Company.

The power-driven revolving doors in the main entrance purred slowly round. You didn't have to push them. You would be foolish to do so: nothing would alter their set speed. You stepped in, adjusted to their pace, and stepped out into the steely blue of the entrance hall with its Italian murals and its symbolic statuary.

'Good morning, Miss Rogers.'

'Good morning.' It was a new messenger who had spoken and she did not know his name, but he knew hers.

One of the six main lifts was waiting. Three men and two women stared straight ahead, conditioned to the idea that the doors would close at an electronically appointed time. Another woman, younger and not yet acclimatised, pressed a button for the fifth floor once, twice and then again. The lift remained unresponsive until Jessica walked in, then its doors closed and it started on its upward journey. At the tenth floor Jessica got out and crossed the corridor to the door marked CAREER DEVELOPMENT FUNCTIONS.

Newcomers often let out a gasp when they opened this door and walked in. The far wall consisted entirely of glass, with a metal stripe across it two feet up from the floor — for visual steadying, said the experts. Beyond the glass was a sprawling, jagged, exhilaratingly jumbled vista of London. The higher you went up this building, the more dizzying the view. From the directors' suites it was difficult, looking down, not to feel that the world lay at your feet — to be divided up or trampled on, as you saw fit.

Jessica was used to the view by now. The girl waiting in the office had evidently not been here before, however, and was gulping nervously and studying the window with unhappy fascination.

'Miss Rogers?' she said, half turning as Jessica came in.

Jessica pulled her desk blotter back from the position into which it was always pushed by the cleaner, and checked that the duplicated copies of the course timetable were waiting in her 'In' tray.

She said: 'You're from Staff Records?'

'That's right.' The girl was dark and pretty, with the slim smartness that Intersyn liked, as though choosing its employees to match the building. 'I've brought the dossiers of the people on the Fifth Executive Course.' Her eyes wandered towards the window again. 'Gosh, don't you get frightened sometimes? It all looks so . . . so close. As though it's tilting up at you.'

'You'll get used to it,' Jessica assured her.

'I'd be afraid of — well, of a storm

breaking the glass . . . of being sucked out . . . or something.'

'It's all been worked out by experts,' said Jessica. 'The worst that can happen to you here is getting a stomach chill from the iced water supply.'

The girl looked blank then forced a giggle. She lifted a large package from the floor and put it on Jessica's blotter. When she peeled the sticky tape from the edge and opened the brown paper, two neatly stacked piles of green-bound dossiers were revealed.

Jessica reached for her check-list.

The girl said: 'Miss Thompson has already checked that they're all complete.'

'We have to be sure,' said Jessica.

'Oh. Oh, yes. Of course.' The girl's giggle got out of hand for a moment. She glanced at the window and glanced away again, gulping. 'Miss Thompson says it's like being the keeper of the Gestapo files.'

After all these years with the Company, thought Jessica, it was time Miss Thompson discarded such fancies. She took out the folders one by one and ticked off the names on her list.

'Do they really keep a record of all of us?' the girl marvelled. 'Absolutely everything about us?'

'They don't have you shadowed once you've left the building in the evening,' Jessica drily reassured her.

'Miss Thompson says you just never know. She says,' the girl chattered on, 'Mr Partridge's nomination is a bit of a surprise.'

'Oh?'

'Well, I don't know, of course — I wouldn't know who she meant — but she says it's someone who's done a parallel Course in the States.'

'Nonsense. Nobody does the Executive Course twice.'

'That's what Miss Thompson says. But she says this time there's one of them . . . Ooh.' The girl spread her feet far apart as though to regain her balance. 'Perhaps I oughtn't to have said . . . '

She certainly ought not to have said anything on those lines. Miss Thompson ought not to have said anything in the first place. The girl might learn in time. Miss Thompson, after all this time,

26

apparently had not learnt. One day her gossipy tongue would carry her too far and she would be quietly informed that she was redundant.

Jessica said: 'Thank you. They all seem to be here.'

The girl went towards the door. From the way she walked one would have thought that the floor sloped upwards and that she was afraid of sliding backwards into infinity.

Jessica studied the green folders, each embossed with a name. Intersyn had no equivalent to the Official Secrets Act, but it was generally understood that people who handled personnel dossiers must be discreet, responsible employees. Annual reports, career assessment record and occasional revealing letters were all bound into these folders. The making or marring of a man was all here.

Miss Thompson ought to be ashamed of herself.

But who was it: who was the man who was doing an Executive Course for the second time; which was Partridge's nomination?

It was none of Jessica's business. Such details were not supplied to the course organisers.

Maybe Partridge simply wanted the man to study the European course for purposes of comparison. But that didn't fit; Partridge was Technical Director of the plant in Yorkshire, and while he was entitled to nominate staff for this gruelling assessment it was not within his province to nose into the methods of personnel handling.

Only once before had there been a nominee who had done a previous Executive Course. It had been before Jessica's time but the story was remembered. A man had been put on the Course knowing every step so well that he could give his undistracted attention to watching somebody else. In fact, he had been appointed to watch the watcher. The management wished to have detailed evidence which would enable them to dismiss the senior lecturer — a damning, detailed, unassailable report. They got it.

A watcher, within the class itself . . .

It could be the same thing all over

again. But watching whom, and for what reason?

The same thing, thought Jessica, all over again.

Poor old Dampier.

Dampier smiled at his class. The tables were large and the chairs reasonably comfortable, but still the grown men before him looked — and, he knew, felt — like small boys on their first day at school. Some of them sat upright and stared boldly at him, asserting their knowledge and self-assurance; but inside they knew that he was their master. If they didn't make a good impression on him he wouldn't cane them or give them lines; but he could put a large or small dent in their career.

He said: 'Please smoke if you wish to. Our fire precautions have been approved by the local authorities.'

There was an eager laugh. He sorted through papers on his desk although he needed no notes, and covertly watched who fumbled too readily for a cigarette, who took his time over lighting a pipe, and who quickly nibbled at a thumbnail.

'Now, gentlemen . . . '

There was an almost audible sigh. His words were the starter's signal.

'These preliminary sessions,' he said, 'will be devoted mainly to the broader aspects of our industry. Each of you is a specialist in his own field, and you may feel as we progress that I am not giving sufficient emphasis to that particular field. If you do, I shall expect you to challenge me at the appropriate time. You may persuade me that I am in error. On the other hand, I may be able to show you that your own job is not quite as all-important as you think. The Company is made up of many interlocking functions. For a day or two I want us to consider the general picture — how those different aspects are all parts of a whole.

'This means that I shall start with the whole problem of the face we show to the world. Because, gentlemen, whether that face is seen clearly or misinterpreted, it *is* the face by which we are judged. Whether you deal with outside contractors or with members of the general public who buy our products or refuse to buy our products, you are giving to them an image of what we are. What we are . . . or think we are . . . or wish people to think we are.

'In other words, let's begin with Public Relations and work our way inwards. Marketing and Public Relations have to be related with technical know-how more than some of us — some of *you* — appreciate.'

It was a routine speech. Dampier knew it off by heart. It gave him the chance to study his pupils while he talked. He smiled as he made one of his little stock of jokes, and let his gaze wander benevolently over the respectful faces. His eyes did not linger anywhere, but he made his first brief assessement. He could always pick out the likely ones. Later he would compare his own opinions with the notes in the dossiers. He was rarely wrong in his first judgment.

It had already been indicated on his list that there were four on whom the management wished to keep a special eye. The little tick against three names meant that here was potential management material — subject, of course, to the findings on the course. The fourth name had a different mark. It did not imply condemnation — unease, rather. It was not that the man was no good: he might well be first-rate in his own field; but they were unhappy. The mark was not a direct invitation to fail the man on the course, but Dampier knew that any plausible failing he could report back would be welcomed. He was skilled at such interpretations.

'Public Relations,' he said, 'is designed to furnish a means of forecasting trends and disseminating information which it is felt desirable to — ah — convey to the public. The public may be a small specialised one or a large general one. In our advertising, our personal contacts and our business relationships we must create an atmosphere of confidence and goodwill which will smooth the way for our salesmen.

'Bleustein-Blauchet, an outstanding figure in French advertising, has defined advertising itself as a conversation between manufacturer and consumer. Our job is to ensure that these are friendly conversations — conversations, that is, which *make* friends . . . '

The phrases came so naturally that he could simultaneously have played a tough game of chess. He hoped there were one or two good chess players on the course. He liked a good fight. This whole course was a fight. The men before him were preparing for a battle for power. It was the same sort of battle as the one he had once fought and from which he had emerged into the profitable peace of his present job. He fed them the right phrases and in the ensuing weeks would see who put them to the best use.

'And allied with the question of our relations with the outside world is the question of internal relations. In many ways our own colleagues and our own employees are our best mouthpieces. If *we* know that what we do is good for the prosperity of humanity, and if we all work together and enjoy working together, we find it much easier to convince customers and newspapers and the most casual contact that Intersyn means well — that

Intersyn works for the benefit of all. Men in senior positions know that the satisfied operative is an operative who has been put in the picture and made to feel that he plays an essential part in the whole design. If our own clerks and typists are dissatisfied with their working conditions, they will tell their friends . . . and this is bad for our image. We have to project the right image. The first discussions on this course will deal with such matters. Some of you may think we are putting the cart before the horse — or, to make the metaphor even clumsier, arranging the transport before we've finalised the product. But experience has shown us that the attitude of our own workers in the plant or in offices conditions what we produce and how we market it. In our discussions we shall work inwards from the outside . . . '

Three or four. There were always three or four on every Executive Course who stood out. It was obvious after the first day who was managerial material. The marks on the official list were usually close, but you got a surprise every now and then: you found the man who had unsuspected talent, who stood out in front of all the others.

And the others — good but not quite good enough. They would spend the rest of their days in cosy jobs, paid better than most of their neighbours yet clawed by a faint resentment, wondering how Jones got ahead and why Smith was now General Manager in Melbourne. The fact that they wondered was proof in itself that they were not of the calibre of Jones and Smith.

Dampier talked, and surveyed his class.

Andrew Flint had a splendid record. Following up the tick on the list, Dampier had skimmed the dossier. Flint was a man who knew where he wanted to go. Whether he would get there or not was a different matter. 'Sensitive about his limited education,' said a note on the file. 'Chip on the shoulder. Excellent at his job but perhaps not suitable for promotion outside his specialised field.' There were later doubts cast on this judgment. Andrew Flint was on the course, so it must be assumed that he was now in the running for promotion. And he had been marked as a favourite.

'I don't want any of you to feel under any restraint during these few weeks,' said Dampier. 'You're not sitting for an examination. I don't mark your papers or recommend that you be expelled.'

Not in so many words. But he knew, and they knew, and he knew that they knew, what his final verdict could mean to them.

'Now, gentlemen. I have done enough talking. I have set the stage, and I think it is high time that you came out and spoke a few pieces on your own behalf. There are twenty of you, and for a day or two we will all have difficulty in remembering names. Intersyn has never believed in the common practice of issuing lapel badges with printed names on them. I think all of us here prefer to think that our personality is sufficient to imprint the name on the consciousness of our colleagues, hm?'

The laughter was still forced and uneasy. One laugh was far too hearty. Dampier made a mental note to check on future sounds from the same source.

'I want you,' he said, 'each to stand up and give a five-minute summary of your career with Intersyn. Don't be too solemn about it. Keep the facts where we can all look at them, and don't feel shy if you haven't done ten years' overseas service. All I want is for us to get to know one another.'

And, he added to himself as automatically as he recited his lines to the class, for me to know exactly what you feel about yourselves. There was always a word or a phrase or an intonation that gave away the truth.

Gerald Hornbrook. Oh, yes — a sure winner. He was smooth and he had been to the right public school. A General Manager in the making. Pleasantly, without undue emphasis, he stood up and outlined his career to date. He had done the right things at the right times. He didn't even have to drop names as some of them always tried so desperately to do. When he did, there was nothing contrived about it. Dampier had met Hornbrook before, under a dozen different names.

He was the perfect Intersyn man. Even when he did not do his job terribly well, he somehow arranged that someone else should do it terribly well for him. He made no wrong decisions. He created a good impression on outside contacts, and even when his staff hated him they felt in a baffled sort of way that he was superior and not to be criticised. If he mentioned the name of a Director and perhaps allowed the implication of a round of golf to creep in — 'As I was saying to Vogel on Saturday afternoon . . . ' — it was quite genuine and unforced. To some of his colleagues this made it worse and even less forgiveable. But the Hornbrooks of this world would always be all right. Dampier knew this and was circumspect in his dealings with them.

'Thank you. And now who shall we have?' He exaggerated the schoolmasterly pomposity, so that they relaxed a little and joined in the joke with him. 'Let me see. Mr Marsh?'

He was younger than most of them. His face was plump and would have been babyish but for the piercing, intense eyes.

Dampier remembered those eyes. The eyes and a certain incongruous determination in the soft, apparently gentle mouth — they were echoes of the boy's father.

David Marsh stood up.

'I joined the Company seven years ago as a marketing trainee. After two years in European Sales Department . . . '

His voice was uncertain yet defiant. There was a crackle in it as though he wished to clear his throat and refused to do so.

It was surprising what people revealed about themselves at this stage. Dampier knew them all — the fluent speaker, the openly boastful, the slyly boastful, the blunt practical men with a scorn for words. Add a point on this side of the balance, two points on that. Nudge this man towards the personnel side, that one back into his sharp-smelling laboratory.

David Marsh talked. Some of his classmates watched him; some doodled on their scrap pads. When he had finished, Dampier felt the jolt that always struck through him when something significant had been done or said.

David Marsh hadn't explained how he came to be with the Company in the first place. Perhaps he didn't want to give the impression that he was a favoured contender, living off a tradition; or perhaps he was afraid of seeming to fawn on the lecturer by expressing gratitude to the Company for all it had done. Either way he was wrong. However he chose to treat the matter it should not have been omitted altogether. It was bound up in the whole concept of Company staff relations which they were discussing and would discuss for several days to come.

Why had Marsh not even mentioned his father?

Dampier realised that the young man was watching him fixedly. He looked nervous yet aggressive, as though daring Dampier to ask a leading question; as though challenging him, thought Dampier indignantly. Silly young fool. Older and more experienced men than he were fully aware that Dampier knew all there was to know.

3

At the end of the first day they left the building as though it was the same for them as for the other thousands pouring out into the street — the end of an ordinary working day. But even those who normally worked here did not, today, hurry towards the car park, the Underground or Liverpool Street Station. They made their way towards the Company hotel just beyond Broad Street.

A large, fresh-faced man looked down at Jessica and boomed at her although they stood only a couple of feet apart. 'Fancy that, now. Letting us find our own way? Not scared we'll get lost or desert, mm?'

She identified him at once as Bill Crowther. He was a bluff, heavy Yorkshireman with a shrewd smile that did not match up with his stentorian voice. She guessed what his approach to the course would be: he would be consistently jovial and make a great show of being a practical man with no time for affectations or wordy nonsense. Some of his associates might regard him as being too coarse and clumsy to succeed. When they discovered their mistake it would be too late.

Jessica said: 'We don't want to shepherd you every minute of the day, Mr Crowther.'

'I thought that was the idea. Never let us out of your sight. Once we're off the leash, how do you know we won't be off on a pub crawl?'

'If you want to go on a pub crawl,' she said, 'it's up to you.'

'And the fact will be duly noted and weighed in the balance, hey?'

Jessica smiled. Crowther grinned knowingly at her and went off towards the street. He shouldered his way through the revolving doors as though determined to make them move faster. But nobody could do that. The doors, the lifts, the mail delivery tubes and the women who brought round morning coffee and pallid afternoon tea — all had their set speeds which nothing could shake or alter.

Some of the Course members were wary. Already, within one day, they felt suspicious of any apparent freedom. They knew they were under surveillance and so they could not believe that they were allowed to walk from one building to another without an escort. This little break in the daily programme had been inserted on the recommendation of an industrial psychologist, but Jessica sometimes felt that the man had been swayed by a neat theory rather than by experience: at this stage the victims were not capable of relaxing. It had been intended that they should feel free to have a drink on the way, to buy an evening paper or to have a stroll round before reaching the hotel. Most of them in fact made straight for the hotel and sat about waiting for the next bell to ring, the next order to be given. Rather than walk the short distance alone, they tended to form groups of three or four.

Andrew left the building alone. He did not hesitate on the pavement outside and he did not glance over his shoulder. He began to walk slowly but steadily towards Finsbury Square.

Jessica had sworn to herself that she would not follow him or go anywhere near him. But already she was making excuses. After all, she had to get to the hotel, too, and this was the quickest way. There was no reason why she shouldn't walk along the opposite pavement. And it was sensible to cross the road at this point; inevitable that their paths should meet on the corner by the pub.

Andrew saw her and frowned.

'Well?' said Jessica as lightly as possible. 'What did you think of your first day?'

'Am I supposed to discuss it with you?'

'You don't have to. We can talk about the weather. Or we can simply stop for a drink.'

'Are you sure you're not doing this under instructions? I don't want to earn myself a black mark.'

'Andrew, you don't think . . . ' She stopped and turned away. She ought to have known better.

He caught her up, reluctantly contrite.

'Jess, we did agree — '

'Yes, I know. I'm sorry.'

'Anyway' — he was bluff and meaninglessly hearty, like a parody of Bill Crowther — 'the club is the place where we drink, isn't it? Surrounded by our fellow back-biters.'

They walked along together, jostled by the rush-hour crowds and occasionally separated by some hurrying, dodging clerk or typist yearning towards a bus stop. Andrew looked straight ahead but she knew that he was alert for anyone from Intersyn who might pass and turn to glance at them.

It had been like this for so long; for what seemed a lifetime. She hardly knew how it had started, and wretched as it was she still could not bear to think that it would ever stop.

She glanced at his set, hard profile. He was a stranger yet closer to her than anyone she had ever known.

In Norwich, her home, there had never been anyone of any importance. Her mother had continually urged the advantages of various boy-friends but they had meant nothing. Jessica had panicked. She wanted to see something of life, to spend at any rate a year or two in a world with wider horizons than those of Norwich. In London she found life more constricted than she had imagined. But there was always the promise of something round the corner. She met a few young men and found them as unsatisfactory as the boy-friends had been. Then she met Andrew. Or, rather, she became gradually aware of Andrew, helping him for a fortnight when his secretary was on holiday, seeing him in the corridors, leaving the building with him and twice having a casual drink with him and somehow casually getting to know him until it was no longer casual. By the time she was fully aware of him it was too late to think rationally about the situation and impossible to turn back.

The affair had matured her. It brought her into assured contact with older and more important men, though none of them had guessed at what was going on. There had been a moment when, being more reckless in the early stages, they had been seen together on the way to her flat.

One flippant comment was enough. Jessica didn't care; but Andrew did. She fell in with his ways, and they made her look older and sadder and in some way more responsible, and thus led to her promotion. Also, in some way she did not understand but dourly recognised, they made her more desirable: men stared at her more than they had done before and pursued her more avidly. But by now she was beyond their reach. Now there was only Andrew.

He said: 'Here we are. The centrally heated goldfish bowl.'

The hotel had been taken over by the Company to provide accommodation for visiting staff from overseas and members of the various training courses. It was also used as a club, with a large bar and an adequate restaurant. It was comfortable and well organised, and from the outside looked like any other hotel, but travellers mistaking it for a place where they might stay or where they might eat before catching a train were politely turned away. The talk in the bar and the lounges and the restaurant was ninety

47

per cent shop talk.

Jessica and Andrew went in together, but Andrew slid discreetly and unobtrusively away and collected his key from the desk. Here there was another difference: you did not sign the register; your name was already entered before you arrived, your room allocated.

Jessica took out one of her lists and checked it against the register.

'All the luggage sent up, Harry?'

'Yes, Miss Rogers.'

'To the right rooms?'

'Of course, Miss Rogers.' The clerk eyed her new dress appreciatively and she knew he would watch her legs when she walked away. There were a lot of jokes about her and about her supposed availability to Executive Course members. She had heard by roundabout ways most of the jokes, including the one about her being a prize for the star pupil on each course. The people who concocted the jokes knew that they were nothing more than fantasies. 'I've put a timetable in each room,' Harry went on, 'and the blank forms for personal details.' Personal details — home addresses and telephone numbers in case one or more of the Course members dropped dead or were driven round the bend by pressure of work. 'Asked them to return 'em to your office by seven o'clock,' said Harry.

'Thank you.'

She was about to turn away when she noticed an alteration on the open page of the register.

'What's this? Two of the room numbers have been changed about.'

'Don't miss a thing, do you, Miss Rogers?'

She saw that Bill Crowther had exchanged rooms with a Philip Western. The name was one of those on her list to which she could not yet fit a face. Within a few days she would know and recognise them all, but at the moment they were still hazy.

She said: 'Was there any special reason for this?'

'Just doing a favour, love — Company good fellowship policy.' It was Crowther, looming over her and thundering amiably. 'Poor lad had a room overlooking the railway. Says he's a bad sleeper, so I swapped with him. Takes a right dive bombing attack to disturb *my* sleep — and even then only if they score a direct hit. Haven't upset the routine, have we?'

'Not at all,' said Jessica. She didn't want to sound fussy by niggling over little points of detail or getting pompous about the sanctity of Company arrangements.

She went up to her rooms on the first floor.

She had a sitting room combined with an office, and beyond it a bedroom. A messenger had already brought the Course dossiers back from the office block and piled them on a corner of her desk. A large timetable was pinned to the green noticeboard on the wall, and a duplicate of the hotel register page was pasted to the desk flap.

Jessica went down the list yet again. The alteration had meant that Philip Western, now in Crowther's allotted room, was next door to Dampier.

She felt a quick pulse begin to beat in her throat. Silly to start imagining things,

50

of course, but . . .

She went through the dossiers and found Western's.

There was no mention in it of his having been on an American course. If he was the spy selected to keep a watch on someone — on Dampier? — his tracks had been well covered. The record was a straightforward one, the sheets of his Company history neatly entered and familiar in layout. Yet she was uneasily conscious that something was wrong. He had done well as Personnel Officer in Brazil, and after a short spell in Canada had come back to handle Job Evaluation and Personnel Relations at the Belby plant. As he had been at Belby some time it was reasonable enough that his recommendation for the Executive Course should have come from Partridge. This was known to Miss Thompson but not recorded in his dossier — assuming that Western *was* the one about whom she had let slip that remark. Miss Thompson could also have known from the staff summary files that Western had done an

American course; but that *ought* to have been in his dossier.

Perhaps it wasn't Western at all. Jessica began to flip quickly through the other folders. She was interrupted two or three times by Course members bringing in their completed personal details forms, looking self-righteous about the speed at which they had done the job.

No; there was nobody in the class who had done the American Course, according to these records. But in going through the folders she suddenly knew what was wrong with Western's dossier. She turned back to it and saw how it was different from the others.

The dossiers were made up of confidential papers and reports covering a number of years. Although all Intersyn offices used the same size and make of paper for staff records, there were faint variations of texture or shade from year to year. As time went by, the edges of one sheet would curl slightly, another would yellow; and there would be variations in the intensity of typewriter ribbon. Western's folder contained sheets which were uniform: and the typing had almost certainly been done at one sitting. It would not have sprung to the eye if you were not looking for it; but once you raised the question, it was obvious.

There was a tap at the door.

'Come in.' Jessica waited for another conscientious student to deliver his completed form.

Dampier's head came round the door. He nodded in the half patronising, half mocking way he had. He adopted this manner towards people who worked for him as opposed to those whom he instructed, as though implying 'we're on the same side, you and I, aren't we?'

Jessica closed the folder.

Dampier raised his eyebrows in an arch grimace. 'Still hard at it, Miss Rogers? No call to exert yourself too hard at the start, my dear — you'll have no energy left for the gruelling later stages.'

'I'm only checking a few details.' She was uneasy, as though she had been caught out in some misdeed. She found it hard to look at him: it would be too much like staring at a condemned man.

'Then stop checking them. It's time we went down to have a drink and' — again his eyebrows worked to emphasise the joke — 'put the poor fellows at their ease.'

As they went downstairs together she wondered if she ought to say something to Dampier. But she had so little to go on. He might pooh-pooh the whole notion, confident that nobody would dare to practise such a deceit on him. If he did take fright and try to ferret out the truth, it would not help him in the long run: they would get him in the end. Better that he should continue with his usual self-assurance unassailed. Better for everyone, really — for the one thing he would certainly do was make trouble for Miss Thompson, the girl, and possibly Jessica herself for gossiping and involving themselves in matters which did not concern them.

The bar was filling up. There were a few women, probably staying in town for the night so that they could go to a theatre: the Company provided four rooms for the use of staff, and these were always booked up weeks ahead. Course members still huddled in groups, not yet confident enough to mix with others. They were anxious not to miss anything that fellow contestants were saying, any hint that might be dropped.

She looked around for Andrew.

★ ★ ★

Andrew saw her come through the doorway and turned quickly to his neighbour.

'Here comes the walking tape recorder. Watch your language!'

The man laughed briefly.

They were supposed to make light sociable conversation showing themselves to be poised men of the world, but the strain of knowing that they were on trial made casual talk impossible. After ten minutes of stuttering half sentences, awkward gaps and feeble flippancies that fell away into nothing, they had all turned inevitably to shop talk.

Someone, anxious to be knowledgeable, told the story of a one-time bright hope who had told an obscene ecclesiastical story to the Bishop of Khartoum at dinner.

55

There was a sudden spurt of conversation. Three separate stories started at once. Everyone knew of some reassuring tale about men who had made fools of themselves in Intersyn's employ. They knew the pitfalls: they weren't going to make similar mistakes.

Then there was a lull, in which a clear voice said: 'You've simply got to get your facts clear if you talk at high levels like I do.' The silence which followed was stunning.

Dampier moved from one cluster to another, gently refusing drinks while urging them to enjoy themselves. Andrew watched him with growing distaste. The man was so damned complacent — a high priest of the Company, accepting their nervous reverence as his due.

'Like *1984*,' muttered a small man with rabbit teeth and spectacles. 'The whole thing fits. Everything done for us — provided we toe the line. And Big Brother beaming at us . . . but ready to snarl at us.'

'They never actually snarl,' remonstrated his companion, the man to whom

Andrew had just spoken and who now looked anxious to dissociate himself from any seditious propaganda.

'I don't approve of this benevolent despot stuff.'

'As long as it's benevolent.'

'Ah, but is it?'

'Well, I'm not one to quarrel with free lunches, a pension, a grant for educating my two boys . . .'

It was the official line, handed out when you joined the Company, set out for your delectation in a glossy handbook. They gave you so many things, and all they asked in return was devout work and loyalty. University graduates received the book cloth-bound; others had card covers.

Andrew moved away as Dampier approached, then hesitated. Better to be there, looking attentive, smiling appreciation of Dampier's smooth sallies. But he felt hostile.

'Flint, isn't it?'

He was confronted by a large man whose name he did not know. Beside him was a younger man whom he remembered as an unsteady, nervous speaker in class — David Marsh.

'I'm Flint,' he agreed. 'Andrew Flint.'

'Bill Crowther. Have a drink?'

'I'm taking it slowly.' Andrew lifted his glass to show that it was half full.

'Aye. Very sensible. I wonder what the Intersyn norm is? It's bad not to drink at all, and bad to drink too much. There wasn't a space for that on the card we had to fill in.'

David Marsh said eagerly: 'Do you suppose the drinks here are supplied by the refinery? Top distillation — that sort of thing.'

Nobody laughed.

'Intersyn,' said Crowther. 'Intestines, my oldest girl calls it. Daddy works for Intestines. Not bad, eh? I always say it's not appropriate: the place is all brains and no guts. Eh . . . mm?'

Andrew had vowed he would be drawn into no careless talk. This was just the sort of meaningless banter that led you into giving yourself away. It was just what they were looking for, in fact. But unless they had planted someone among the Course members to report back, who would know what was being said at this moment in this corner? Dampier was out of earshot. Maybe they had got the place wired. No: even Intersyn would surely not go that far.

'Computers,' Crowther proceeded. 'How can you make decisions about men with computers? Time and motion study, and all the rest of it — no heart to it.'

'Time and motion study,' said Andrew stiffly, 'is carried out with every regard to the individual human being.'

Dampier moved closer, his eyes wandering, his smile fixed and reflective.

Crowther said: 'But the individual gets lost once the figures are fed into a machine. All the welfare schemes and the personnel development schemes and the rest of it — all worked out in little squiggles and holes in cards from data fed into a mess of metal, glass and wire.'

'Not forgetting Intersyn plastics,' added young Marsh.

'Fed in,' said Andrew, 'by expert personnel men.'

'Experts,' said Crowther, 'with the minds of computers.'

Dampier was not so much listening to them as waiting to be asked to do so. He stood with his head slightly back, certainly hearing every word but politely waiting for one of them to catch his eye and include him in the conversation.

Andrew said: 'The advantage of computers is that they work objectively, uninfluenced by emotion or fallible personal judgments. There's no old-boy network built into them.' He stopped, aware that this could sound aggressive. He must not give the impression of having a chip on his shoulder. Theoretically there was equal opportunity for all in the Company. He changed his approach. 'They can deal more swiftly with staff problems than the most conscientious personnel officer could hope to do. They have no prejudices — '

'And no heart,' said Crowther.

'Irrational emotions, you mean?'

'Heart is what I mean,' said Crowther bluntly. 'When I joined this Company we all knew one another. Even when it started to grow, we all kept in touch and felt we belonged to the same family. When there were marriages we had parties, and when we went to associated companies overseas we could drop in on old pals and chat, and swap stories, and pass on the news.'

'Taking up hours of valuable working time,' Andrew jibed.

'We got the job done. Better than anyone does now, if you ask me. And when someone was in trouble, the Company helped. I'm not saying it doesn't now — '

'I should hope not. Consideration shown towards employees undoubtedly improves work output.'

'Ahhh!' Crowther produced a twisted, rasping sound from deep in his throat. 'That's just the trouble. That's the way it is now. That's the whole modern attitude. But it wasn't like that in the old days. I could tell you a dozen stories to prove it wasn't. I remember when we flew four kids out to Bombay — not because it was in a contract or because it would affect the output one tiny little bit, but just because it made the wife of one of our lads happy. And there was old Johnson's illness: you couldn't have worked out a plan for that just by feeding job breakdowns into a machine. And that young chap, whatever his name was — lad whose father had an accident while he was up at the plant. All his own fault, they said. Proved it, in fact. But the Company didn't just make a quiet settlement and forget it all. They gave the youngster a good education, looked after his mother, and then took him on and did everything they could for him.'

Despite himself Andrew said: 'One of those vague goodwill tales. Probably put out by Public Relations Section.'

'Oh, no,' said Dampier, taking the two steps that made him part of the group. 'No, it's true enough. Isn't it, Mr Marsh?'

David Marsh flushed. 'Yes. Quite true.'

Andrew felt himself flushing too: a deeper, angrier red than young Marsh. Why the hell hadn't the young fool stopped him — why had he let him go on?

Crowther guffawed. 'Put both your big feet right in it, Flint! Never mind — always doing it myself. Makes a change to see someone else in up to the knees.'

Andrew forced a laugh. There was an awkward silence.

A shrill voice from a group nearby floated into their oasis of stillness. 'Holidays? Good heavens, I haven't an idea. I just haven't been able to fix anything — I've been far too busy to look at the list.'

'What time is dinner?' said someone else, doggedly overriding a buzz of conversation. 'I've been having nothing but sandwich lunches just lately. I find it better when I'm hard pressed . . . '

Crowther said: 'Well, we'd better stop chipping away at the Company. There'll be no salary increases for us this year if we get too nasty.'

'If employees were marked down for disloyal remarks,' said Dampier amiably, 'we would have a cheap year this year. Or,' he added with a twinkle, 'any other year.' His long arm curled out slowly but purposefully, and without effort was drawing Jessica into the circle. 'Jessica, my dear. You'll join us for a drink?'

She glanced fleetingly at Andrew with

that shy, long-lashed, unhappy look of hers. Nobody else would know it, but she was asking his permission. He did not respond.

She said: 'Thank you, but I was on my way out. I think I'll have a stroll before dinner.'

'In the wicked streets of the City?' said Dampier archly.

'The deserted streets of the City,' said Jessica.

As she went she passed close to Andrew. At least she had the sense this time not to look at him, but she was appealing to him to follow her. And she knew he wasn't going to.

David Marsh said: 'You know, that's not a bad idea. Short constitutional after a tough day. Give one an appetite.'

He waited until Jessica had left the bar and then went off in the same direction. Dampier watched him go and chuckled.

'Aha! It seems that the fair Jessica has made another conquest.'

'Pretty girl,' said Crowther. 'A nice lass.'

'Most efficient. And, as you say, pretty.

A few hearts always have to be swept up at the end of each course. But' — there might have been a warning note in his voice, though it was now too late to reach young Marsh — 'I think Miss Rogers is too sensible to become involved in any emotional entanglements arising from the somewhat unnatural conditions in which you gentlemen have to work for the next few weeks.'

Andrew hoped that he was not showing his anger. It burned away inside him with an added, unexpected intensity. Young Marsh had no business to be on this Course and no business to be sniffing after Jess so quickly and blatantly. He was too young for the course and too young for Jess. A charity case, pushed forward beyond his capabilities by the benevolent Company . . . and still adolescent in his petty little itch for a woman who was far beyond his understanding.

Alcohol was slackening the tongues all around him. Loquacious boasts began to seethe up, splintered by loud, self-congratulatory laughter.

'Yes, I had three or four offers of much

higher salary, but I accepted Intersyn as a challenge . . . '

'I always find that if I take a tape recorder home for the weekend it's so much easier for me to get a few thoughts put down . . . '

Andrew looked resolutely into his empty glass, waiting for the tight knot of rage inside him to slacken. He heard Crowther's voice booming beside him. It was not until the question was asked for the third time that he realised Crowther was offering to refill his glass.

★   ★   ★

There were still a few late workers leaving their offices, and there were heads against the frosted glass of pub windows — the heads of commuters who had missed their trains or who were simply reluctant to go and catch the trains. Apart from them, the City was slowing down into its nightly tranquillity. The streets were already almost deserted. Within another hour the buses would weave between the tall banks and insurance offices and sooty churches with only a few passengers aboard.

Jessica slowly crossed a street that in the daytime would be jammed with traffic. She stopped to look idly in the window of a bookshop. After a moment or two she saw a hazy reflection drifting towards her, distorted by the bright jackets of the books beyond the glass.

David Marsh said: 'I do hope you don't mind . . . that is, if you'd sooner be on your own . . . I just felt rather like a saunter, and there you were, and . . . well . . .'

Her immediate impression of him was that of a boy in his Sunday best. He was a boy who had suddenly shot up, outgrown his clothes, and been bought more clothes of which he was inordinately careful. She had noticed earlier today how he frequently adjusted his tie so that it hung straight instead of twisting under his jacket, and how he checked that his pocket flaps were not tucked in or creased. He was neat and nervous and on his best behaviour. She thought that he had been sent on this course before he was ready for it.

'It'll be nice to have someone to talk to,' she said.

They fell into step and walked at a leisurely pace towards the Monument. She took him down a narrow alley into a square impregnated with the cooking smells from an ancient chop-house, and he was delighted. He knew little of the by-ways of the City.

'But it's all so quiet,' he marvelled. 'By tonight we'll be the only people alive round here, won't we?'

'There's certainly not much going on after half past six or seven o'clock,' Jessica agreed. 'That's why we had to take over the hotel. When the new building went up, the L.C.C. made recommendations about social club facilities and living accommodation — they're beginning to insist that business houses can't just pull employees in during the day and then leave the place desolate at night. The same with the South Bank, I believe: they want some sort of community life in the area during the evenings. So Intersyn is gallantly trying to bring back song, dance and jollity to the City.'

'I never knew that before. About the regulations, I mean.'

A burglar alarm went off somewhere above their heads, clanked for a minute or so as they passed, and was then abruptly cut off. No policeman appeared. No whistles sounded, no shouts of alarm. A newspaper delivery van and a bus hooted spitefully at each other and then moved apart. A torn page of *The Financial Times*, trapped in the grid of a drain, twitched slowly and turned pulpy as water trickled along the gutter into it.

Jessica said: 'You haven't been in Central Office for long?'

'Only a few months. They've shunted me about in the backwoods for most of my time.'

'Building up practical experience, we call it,' she smiled.

'That's the story.' He took her arm to halt her on a corner as a heavy lorry rattled round. His touch was unsure yet commanding. 'A complete education, fitting me for high responsibility. My father used to say . . . ' He bit off the last word. His grip tightened, although the lorry had gone.

'Your father . . . ?' she prompted.

He urged her across the road and his hand fell away as they reached the opposite pavement. 'Nothing,' he said. Then he said: 'You know about my father, of course.' Before she could reply, he went on: 'You must know everything about everybody on this Course.'

Jessica had experienced many attempts to get her to talk. On every Course there was at least one man who tried to pump her. She was not sure whether David Marsh was clumsily attempting this or whether he was really as innocent as he looked.

Innocent . . . She realised with a shock that he was not quite the gauche young man he had at first appeared to be. Since the moment when he mentioned his father, his eyes had clouded and there were little puckered lines of pain at the corners of his eyes and mouth.

Uneasily she turned their footsteps back in the direction of the hotel.

At the entrance he said: 'Oh, heavens. I forgot to hand in that card — the one with the personal particulars.'

'That's all right. It'll do first thing in — '

'I've filled it in,' he hastened to assure her, 'but I left it on my dressing table. I'll dash up straight away and get it. I'll bring it to your office before we go down to dinner.'

'I pass your room on my way along,' said Jessica. 'I can pick it up on the way.'

They reached the desk. Harry was already holding Jessica's key out to her, dangling from his little finger. He looked enquiringly at David Marsh.

David said: 'Er — Room 205.'

Harry scanned the hooks, then shook his head. 'Not here, sir.'

David blinked, and put his hand in his pocket.

'A bit bulky to carry about, sir,' said Harry.

'I can't have dropped it. Must have left it in the door.' He patted both pockets again and stared past Harry at the board as though hoping to conjure the key back into its rightful place. 'That's a bad beginning!'

Jessica went upstairs and along the landing with him. The key was indeed where he had left it, in the door.

Tomorrow, thought Jessica abstractedly, he would probably find as he started to take notes in the classroom that he had omitted to refill his fountain pen. And he would lose some of the papers from his folder; perhaps even the folder itself, either here or on the way to the Belby plant. Left to his own devices, he might miss the train or get the wrong one. There was always one candidate like David — one man who got flustered and lost things, did things wrong, lost his grip.

He opened the door and went in.

'Just a tick. Let you have the card.'

She was outside the door but she saw him jolt to a stop. He stood quite still in the middle of his room, staring. Through the crack of the door she could catch the glint of his dressing table mirror.

She said: 'Anything wrong?'

There was a pause. Then he said, 'No,' very slowly.

He turned to look at the chest of drawers immediately inside the door.

From it he picked up the card and studied it for a moment.

'I could have sworn . . . '

Then he shook his head and handed the card to Jessica.

The dinner gong throbbed from the hall below. Jessica took the card and went on to her room.

Stopping in the middle of his room as he had done, David Marsh had looked like a startled animal — an animal suddenly alerted to danger, sensing something in the wind. It was as though he had at once reacted to a change in the place. Someone was in the room . . . or had been in the room.

The card that ought to have been on the dressing table had been on the chest of drawers. Unless, of course, he had got it all wrong. He had forgotten, just as he had forgotten about his key.

Jessica thoughtfully consulted her list once more, half knowing what she would find. David's room was on the far side of Philip Western's from Dampier. Western was between the two of them. Western could have searched David's room in mistake for Dampier's.

Unless it was all a silly fancy, a lurid twist of her imagination . . .

David Marsh had left his key in the door. He was nervous, flustered by the solemnity of the Executive Course, unsure of himself and his surroundings. It was much more likely that, forgetting his key, he was also liable to forget where he had put the personal particulars card.

But in her mind's eye she still saw the rigidity of his back, the tense alertness of him.

4

'And now,' said Dampier on the eighth day of the Course, 'we come to our brainstorming session.' He smirked like a benevolent torturer about to demonstrate the therapeutic qualities of a thumbscrew. 'We call it Operation Cammanplan — Campaign and Management Planning.'

He went on to explain. It was an explanation that invariably produced a wide range of expressions on the faces of his class. Some looked baffled, some apprehensive, others faintly derisive. They would all go into it with the feeling that they were playing a game; but it was remarkable how quickly the game gripped them and how worked up they could get about it.

Dampier said: 'You will be divided into four teams of five, each with a leader. Each team will be shut away in one of our smaller rooms and left to work out a problem which I will set. This is an exercise in group dynamics. As you probably know, 'war games' have always been a feature of the training in military staff colleges, and for a long time now we have found it useful to play a 'management game'. I want you to suppose that you are planning a major expansion in some African country which has recently achieved independence. I will give each of you a list of snags which have to be overcome, and from those snags you will have to deduce what other difficulties there may be. You will have the whole day in which to work out a campaign — that is, a sales campaign preceded by a Public Relations drive and by supply planning. I may say that I shall be much more interested in the way you tackle the Public Relations aspect than in the mere shifting of material from one country to another.'

He studied their attentive faces. Yes, there was the beginning of a controlled sneer over there: Andrew Flint, hardly able to repress his contempt for this classroom frivolity, was settling back wearily in his chair. And Crowther was openly grinning. Gerald Hornbrook, on the other hand, had a twitch of smugness about his lips. This was the sort of game he had been accustomed to playing in real life.

'I will appoint four leaders,' said Dampier. 'Each leader will be regarded, for the sake of the exercise, as a General Manager. When you are shut away in your cells, he will appoint a Public Relations Officer, a Sales Manager, a Finance Manager, and a Production and Transport Manager.'

And it will be interesting, he added to himself, to see what choices the leaders make. Their selective ability would play a big part in his own final assessment of them.

They were very still and attentive. He knew what they were waiting for. They were in their second week and they knew he would have formed opinions of them all by now. They wanted to see how those opinions were reflected in his choice of the four men to lead the brainstorming teams.

Deliberately he kept them waiting a few

minutes longer. He continued smoothly:

'You must regard yourselves as competing companies. You will be asked to assume that you all stand an equal chance at the beginning — but the later stages will depend largely on how you tackle the problem of persuading the President or Prime Minister or dictator of the new country that you should be allowed commercial freedom. Halfway through the day I shall come to each of you and — I promise you — find some way of upsetting each plan so that you will have to readjust quickly to new circumstances, perhaps revising your whole campaign, perhaps managing with only a few swift changes . . . perhaps deciding to abandon the whole thing. Twenty minutes will represent two months in the life of your Company. Now . . . ' He consulted a sheet of paper on his desk, although his choice of names was already made. 'The leaders,' he said.

A match spluttered harshly along the matchbox and Crowther lit his pipe. Another man stubbed out a half-smoked cigarette.

'Mr Flint will lead one team,' said Dampier. Heads turned towards Flint in rueful congratulation. Nobody was surprised that his name should have come up. 'And . . . let me see . . . '

The more subtle among them would by now be wondering whether the choice of leaders was as significant as it might appear. How could they be sure that Dampier wasn't choosing at random, simply to put them on their mettle — or, even if he was naming the four most promising pupils, that he wasn't giving them the chance of making a hideous mess at this stage and thereby demoting themselves? They couldn't be sure.

He said: 'Mr Hornbrook.'

Of course. Hornbrook acknowledged the nomination with a slight but confident nod. Nobody would have been more surprised than Hornbrook himself if he had not been selected.

'Mr Ames.'

That shook them. Ames had made no great showing so far and was one of the least conspicuous members of the class. But he might surprise them. He was one of the quiet, dogged type with a primly organised mind: he might be no great personality in himself, but it was possible that he had the ability to bring out and organise all that was best in his subordinates. That was what Dampier wished to find out.

'And . . . ' He hesitated. They were all fairly sure that he was about to nominate Crowther. Crowther's deep-browed concentration on the tamping down of smouldering tobacco in his pipe bore witness to his own conviction on this score.

Dampier said: 'Mr Western.'

Crowther did not look up. His neighbour glanced at him but obtained no response. Crowther drove his middle finger down into the bowl of his pipe, withdrew it in a blackened state, and struck another match.

'And now for the teams,' said Dampier.

He proposed to give the self-effacing Ames a strong team and to see what he made of them. Hornbrook . . . yes, Hornbrook must have Crowther as one of his group; they would inevitably clash, and it would be interesting to see whether the outcome was fruitful or destructive.

Then there was Flint. As a time and motion study expert, he would undoubtedly have his team sorted out and getting on with the work in five minutes flat. He would probably turn in the most professional, foolproof result — sound rather than inspired. There would be no clumsy flaws in Flint's end product; unless, that is, he was provided with an irritant to throw him off his carefully calculated course.

Dampier contemplated David Marsh. It would be rewarding to put those two together. Already they had had two somewhat acrimonious arguments in class. There was a bristling antipathy between them that had its origins outside the Course. Young Marsh spent rather too much of his time in the restaurant, the bar, and the streets between this building and the hotel, in the company of Jessica. And Dampier was most interested to observe that Andrew Flint didn't like this. Most interested. Flint took no overt steps to do anything about the situation; but certainly he didn't like it.

Dampier said, 'In Mr Flint's team, I think we should have Mr Blackwell . . . Mr Marsh . . . '

Flint started, then glared at him, then looked alarmed. It was beginning to dawn on Flint that the lecturer knew or guessed more than he ought to do. They were all the same, in every class on every Course: they were like children who were continually taken by surprise, continually surprised to find themselves under such keen, adult observation. They thought they could hide things; but it was difficult to hide anything from Dampier.

He added three more names to Flint's team and turned his attention to Western. It was only now that he realised, with a twinge of annoyance, that Western's response when his name was announced had been a peculiar one. Dampier had seen his reaction without quite registering it. It might almost have slipped past him. But now he remembered that Western had shown no gratification — that there had, in fact, been a fleeting furrow of displeasure on his brow. It was as though he didn't want the chance to prove himself. To him it was nothing more than a nuisance, in some way an interference.

Significant . . . but of what?

★ ★ ★

Andrew sat at the head of the table and tried to concentrate.

He was in no mood for playing games. He knew that this was a crucial stage in the screening process that was going on every hour of every day for these six weeks and that it demanded his full attention, but his resolves were being undermined. The planting of David Marsh on him had been deliberate. There was no shadow of a doubt about that. And there was no doubt whatsoever about the reasons.

He shuffled the papers on the table before him. It was all too easy to conjure up a picture of the fussy, gleeful little men who had concocted these posers and fake figures. They must have had some happy hours inventing the politics of their mythical African country.

Yet he had started out knowing that this whole Course was a protracted game. He had gone into it determined to play hard and to win.

Now all he could think about was Jessica. Jessica and that baby-faced young upstart. He ought to have been pleased: Marsh had been openly spending too much time with Jessica, and Marsh had not been appointed leader of a team; but instead of justifying his whole approach to the Course and providing a stimulus it was proving a distraction.

He forced himself to speak.

'We are proposing to set up a sales organisation in Nogoland.' And what little dimwit had hugged himself when he dreamed up *that* name? 'We are faced with some opposition from the new Government, who came to power on slogans of shaking off colonial rule and building up local crafts, industries and commerce. First we have to produce a new climate of opinion. We have to make it clear that we wish to play a part in the country's prosperity and that we have no intention of exploiting it selfishly. We want to lead up to the establishment of good trading relations and then to the construction of an assembly plant for prefabricated sections and bulk supplies shipped from the United Kingdom or France. Starting with stories fed to the local Press about the beneficial results of our international operations . . . '

Plastic buckets for Peru, petroleum chemical derivatives for industry in Africa and Asia, lighting insulation for a million electrical fitments — they were all part of the Intersyn boast, repeated over and over again in all possible media of publicity. How could the familiar, practised techniques be most effectively applied to this new situation?

He said: 'The first thing is to get our Public Relations Officer moving. I think that's the job for you, Marsh.'

'Oh.' David Marsh cleared his throat. 'Actually, P.R. isn't my strong subject. I've done most of my work on the marketing side. I think I'll be more use to the team if I stick to that.'

'As I understand it,' said Andrew ominously, 'this Course is designed to put people in difficult situations and see how they respond, so that the Company can assess the calibre of its employees. So I'm appointing you P.R. Officer. All right?'

Marsh had gone pale. He could not take a reproof. He had no business to be on this Course at all.

'All right.' His voice was tight and steady.

'Good. Now, let's spend the first quarter of an hour working out our P.R. campaign. Sales, Finance' — he quickly nodded his three remaining choices — 'and Production and Transport. Finance will have to come first. These papers here give details of budget allocations. I want you to let me know how much we can set aside for our preliminary campaign.'

They discussed the matter slowly and self-consciously at first but the Sales and Finance boys were soon enthusiastic. Like a reluctant group dragged into charades at a party they began to throw themselves into it. Only Marsh remained uncomfortable. He floundered. His suggestions were lame and uncreative. The project did not even get off the ground until they left the

P.R. campaign, assuming that it had done its job — a risky assumption — and went on to more practical matters. Here Marsh's contributions were sound enough, but Andrew did not accept many of them. Although he tried to be objective, he instinctively slapped Marsh down at every possible opportunity. With one part of his mind he knew that this would do the team no good and that the results of their debate would be open to criticism by Dampier; but with another part he enjoyed jabbing and stabbing at the awkward, amateurish young man.

Dampier came in at the halfway mark and studied their achievements so far. He looked once at Andrew with an expression mingling surprise and speculation, and then briskly told them that something had gone wrong. A competitor had obtained a prior concession; after a board meeting in London their budget had been cut by one third; and in the light of new developments they must institute a new campaign in half the time originally planned.

'I leave you with it, gentlemen,' said

Dampier, and left them with it.

It ought to have been engrossing. But Andrew could not channel all his energies into this struggle. He had known about the game before he joined the Course and had looked forward to it. Then, today, the mere sound of it had been ridiculous, and now that he was plunged into it he simply could not concentrate.

Young Marsh got on his nerves. So did the sleek Hornbrook, who at this moment was probably evolving a nice, sleek, civilised programme. Last weekend in the bar he had snapped loudly at Hornbrook, who had of course been quite unruffled. Last weekend — drinking in the bar and putting on the Intersyn act instead of being with Jessica. He *could* have arranged to spend a couple of hours with her. She had been at the flat all weekend — she slept in the hotel only during the week, unlike the imprisoned competitors — and there had been that free period on Sunday afternoon when he could have got to her. She would have been so pleased. Or would she? He tried to remember whether

Marsh had been in the hotel that afternoon or whether he had gone out for one of those supposed strolls of his.

Damn it, they didn't have to be prisoners — or, worse still, children kept in a barred room. If he asserted himself and refused to agree to the more ridiculous rules of the Course, might that not be regarded as a sign of decisiveness? Might the Company not be waiting to see who would be the first to show that kind of courage and independence?

And quite apart from that, he wanted to get out anyway.

He looked at Marsh's head, bowed over the table in contemplation of a distribution agency map, and wondered if Marsh had been to Jessica's flat yet. He was sure Jessica wouldn't have invited him so soon. Sure that she would never invite him. Sure. Sure that he was being stupid in falling prey so easily to jealousy.

'Mr Flint. If our rivals have port facilities while we have to build a new jetty . . . '

'Mm?'

'The port. There are only two in

Nogoland, and one of them has fallen into disuse because of the silting up of the harbour entrance. That's what we've been told, anyway.'

'Yes, yes,' said Andrew tetchily. 'Get on. What are you proposing?'

They finished the game and finished the day. Dampier took half an hour to sum up the results of their efforts, and announced that Western's team had won, with Flint's coming in second. Andrew's cloud of gloom lifted slightly. He had not expected this. It must have been due entirely to the labours of his Sales and Finance nominees.

'I have put Mr Flint's group second,' said Dampier, 'in spite of the unevenness of many of their findings. I'll discuss these in more detail tomorrow, as the subject is a most interesting one — the effectiveness of certain brilliant strokes in spite of an overall untidiness.'

With better leadership, thought Andrew, there wouldn't have been that untidiness. He surreptitiously studied Western's craggy, arrogant features. Here evidently was a serious rival. From now on there could be no slacking; no time for luxurious self-pity or self-doubt.

In the bar that evening there was a hubbub of eager discussion. Most of them were continuing to play the Cammanplan game, exchanging jokes and arguments.

'When old Dampier came in and mucked up our plan with that stinker of a setback . . . '

'Harry came out with one glorious remark in the middle of it . . . '

Some of them were by now on Christian name terms. Others remained suspicious and aloof, snapping out surnames with military impersonality.

'I used to attend Monty's conferences at Eighth Army,' said a tall man with a crisp moustache, 'and I know.'

'I wanted to go to New York last autumn but unfortunately I was two executive levels too high for the conference. Silly, isn't it?'

And a persistent echo from an earlier evening, 'I've accepted Intersyn as a challenge.'

'Harry came out with a gorgeous one . . . '

Andrew realised that he was already on his third drink. He looked round the bar. There was no sign of Jessica. But at least Marsh was here, talking to someone.

Andrew went on drinking until dinner-time. The babble of argument hardly slackened during the meal. Afterwards he made his way back to the bar and took up where he had left off. It was some little time before he noticed that David Marsh was now not in the room.

He edged his way through the crush towards the door which led into the lounge.

The room beyond was equipped with leather-covered easy chairs, tables and newspaper racks. A desk in one corner was supplied with Company headed paper. A man was bent over it, writing assiduously. Two of the walls were lined with bookshelves. The Executive Course members made little use of this: it was meant more for the Technical Courses which passed through twice a year.

Jessica was seated at a table in the middle of the room, turning over the pages of a magazine. There were two other chairs at her table, empty.

Andrew stood over her. 'All alone?'

'Not quite,' said a suave voice behind him.

Western and Marsh had been standing at one of the bookshelves. They came towards the table and sat down in the two chairs. Western smiled up at Andrew. He had thin lips that were too fine and colourless for his broad jaw. Andrew stood awkwardly over them, in what ought to have been a commanding position but wasn't. He waited for Jessica to acknowledge his presence. She was about to speak when Western said to David, markedly continuing a private conversation:

'I hadn't realised you had such a grasp of the technical processes. Not many of our Marketing chaps have that kind of background.'

'It's not essential. You don't have to understand chemical reactions to be able to sell the finished product.'

'No, but one would have thought that if that was your bent you would have made a career in the plant. Why aren't you one

93

of the Belby boys?'

'There are reasons,' said David Marsh. His right eye half closed in a slight tic, as though he had a lazy eye. 'Reasons of state, you might say.'

Jessica looked at Andrew and looked away. She reached for her glass from the table, sipped at it, and yawned.

Andrew turned and went out of the room, back to the bar.

Later, when he looked into the lounge again, all three of them had gone. Early to bed? And to whose bed?

He tried to wrench his thoughts out of this pattern. The hell with Jessica and the hell with Marsh. Petty jealousy and petty spite weren't going to help him on this Course. From tomorrow on he would control his imaginings. He would win. He had to win.

When he went to bed there were few men left in the bar. His mouth felt dry and sour. He drank three glasses of water, gagging on the third.

At the end of a sleepless hour he found that he must go to the lavatory.

On the way back he stopped at the end

of the corridor and looked along it. The lights looked bleak at this time of night — or, rather, morning — like the hazy, acrid lights of a dismal railway station. The doors were all closed and nothing moved. Somewhere outside, a world away, an engine clanked hollowly across points and then there was silence. Andrew was about to turn away when he noticed a gleam of light from one of the doors. At first he thought it must be partly open, then realised that the light was reflecting from a key left in the lock of the door.

He walked quietly along the corridor. It was David Marsh's room. He knew that: he had already shamefacedly checked on the numbers and the distance between this room and Jessica's. They were not far enough apart.

He wondered if Jessica were inside.

That was ridiculous. Of course she wouldn't come to Marsh's room.

Yet she would have been willing to come to Andrew. She had wanted to. Before the Course started she had pestered him to let her come, or at least that he should come to hers.

But it couldn't have got that far with Marsh yet. Jess wasn't that kind of girl.

A woman scorned . . .

Oh, the hell with it. It was absurd. He knew her too well. He was the only man she wanted.

And when she couldn't get him . . . ?

There was a good excuse for knocking. He could knock and bring Marsh to the door, pointing out the risks of leaving his key in the lock; could edge his way in or provoke Marsh into giving something away.

It was flimsy but it was an excuse. It would do.

Andrew wavered. Then he went on past the room, round the corner and towards Jessica's rooms.

The outer door was slightly ajar. He debated whether to knock. But if she were alone she wouldn't mind if he walked right in. Whenever he arrived unexpectedly at her flat he had only to let himself in and walk into the sitting room or the kitchen or the bedroom, and she would spin round to welcome him like a child welcoming an unforeseen treat.

And if she weren't alone . . .

Andrew pushed the door open and went in.

A cluster of signal lights rearing above the chasm of the railway cast a glow across the office desk. Then a shadow moved across the window and came swiftly at Andrew. He put up one arm instinctively and backed away a pace. A fist hammered into his jaw. He lurched sideways, trying to regain his balance, and his head cracked against the edge of the open door.

As he reeled into blackness he was hit again — twice, three times — and then he was falling and seemed to go on falling with no sensation of hitting the floor.

5

When he came round, Jessica was saying: 'Andrew . . . what happened? Andrew!'

He reached out as though hoping to find the bed safe beneath him, the sheets and blankets tucked in around him. Instead, he was stiff, lying at an awkward angle on a hard floor, and his head was being pounded to bits from inside and outside at the same time.

'Andrew.'

There was panic in her voice and yet she sounded drowsy. He wanted to reassure her but found it difficult to form the words.

'I'm all right,' he mumbled. Even that much effort hurt.

Her arm was about his shoulders. She helped him to sit up. He winced.

'What happened?' she said again. She had hardly finished speaking when she was overtaken by a massive yawn. She was still sleepy, her voice slurred.

Andrew shook his head then wished he hadn't done. But he was wide awake all right. He said:

'Your boy-friend bumped into me on his way out.'

'What are you raving about?'

'I'm amazed he had that much energy. He certainly packs a hard punch.'

'Raving,' said Jessica. 'You're raving. You must be.'

The languorous voice was so familiar. He had heard it so often, drugged with sated passion, the sleepy aftermath of lust.

He said: 'He was here, wasn't he? You ought to be more careful. Or you ought to teach him to be. Not even closing the door properly behind him. You never know who might walk in. Look who did walk in, in fact.'

She was making an effort to wake up thoroughly. 'I don't know what you're talking about. Nobody has been here. I've been asleep.' Again she yawned. 'I feel so . . . so doped.'

'Doped?' It was meant as a sneer, but changed into a question.

'I've been sleeping like a log. I felt so dizzy downstairs, and as soon as I got up here I went flat out. Hardly had time to get into my pyjamas. I just' — her head sagged — 'collapsed.'

Andrew struggled to his feet and swayed for a moment. Jessica put out an arm to steady him but was not much steadier herself.

'Who were you drinking with?' he demanded.

'You know. You saw me. David — David Marsh. And that man Western.'

'And who saw you to your room?'

'David,' she said defiantly.

'Very clever. He gave you too much to drink and brought you back here.' He was accusing her rather than Marsh. 'And then what?'

'Then nothing,' she retorted. 'I've told you. I was just about able to get myself into bed. I didn't hear another thing until you woke me. I heard a terrific thump out here. I didn't really take it in — I woke up and then started to drift off to sleep again — but you must have moaned or something, because I felt I had to crawl out of bed and come and see what was going on.'

He stumbled towards the door and switched the light on. It struck their eyes like a savage blow. Jessica put up an arm to shield herself from the glare. She looked pathetic and defenceless. In some way it stimulated his anger. He wanted to strike her simply because she was so defenceless; because she was asking for it.

'You can't tell me you didn't want young Marsh to come to your room. And you can't tell me he didn't want to. And if he gave you too much to drink, what other reason — '

'No.' She was being jarred into wakefulness at last. 'No. Nothing happened. Neither of us is ready for anything to happen . . . yet.'

'Yet?' he echoed.

'Andrew, please — we don't want the whole hotel woken up.'

He still had enough control over himself to recognise the truth of this. The Course was still important to him. He had meant not to see Jessica, not to come to her while the Course lasted. He had

101

slipped a long way since making that resolve; but he was not going to ruin the whole thing. They went on in tense, angry whispers.

'Just what goes on between you and young Marsh?'

'Nothing that we're ashamed of.'

'Nobody's talking about shame. You can go a long way without being ashamed.'

'I've certainly done pretty well in the last couple of years,' she admitted.

'What do you mean by that?'

'I think you know.'

'If you're implying — '

'I'm not implying anything. But I don't think you have any cause for complaint, Andrew. You've neglected me; you don't want to have anything to do with me while you're on this Course, and God knows if you'll condescend to have anything to do with me afterwards; and yet you're suspecting me of having an affair with somebody else, and actually getting jealous about it. I suppose I should be flattered.'

'Jess, you're making yourself cheap.'

'Am I?' she marvelled. 'Then perhaps that's the real me.'

'You know it isn't.'

'I don't know. I have so little idea what I really am. But I do know' — her whisper became sharp and cutting — 'I'm not going to be one man's property any longer. Particularly when he can't be bothered to use his property more than once every three or four weeks.'

'Next thing,' he lashed out, 'you'll be going off for romantic weekends with that youngster.'

'Possibly.'

She turned her head up to the light now and blinked her eyes like a haughty cat.

He said: 'What do you mean by that?'

She shrugged.

'The weekend before we go to Belby!' he accused her. 'He's invited you to go away with him. That's it, isn't it?'

'I haven't had any other invitations, so there's no reason why I shouldn't accept.'

'You'd be bored stiff. You'll probably be bored to tears by him before we even reach that weekend.'

'Let's wait and see, shall we? He's invited me,' she added, 'to meet his mother — to stay with them down at Maidenhead.'

'Serious stuff, hey?' Andrew mocked her.

'Now perhaps you'll go.'

An early morning despair settled on both of them. They had been staring into each other's eyes as they talked, each trying to make the other flinch with the whispered thrusts. Now they stood apart and could not look at each other.

Jessica said: 'My desk . . . '

Andrew followed the direction of her gaze. There were files open on the desk. Two neat piles of folders stood at one side, and there were three opened, with a couple of timetables lying across them. One of the desk drawers was half open.

'Something wrong?' he said grudgingly.

'Someone's been tampering with the files.'

'Now look, Jess, there's no need to dream up a nice cover story — '

'Go,' she said. 'Go back to bed. Please.

I've had enough.'

He knew he had gone too far. He knew, also, that she was sincere.

'Jess, if there's really been something going on in here . . . if you were really doped so that there was time for someone to go through your papers . . . Look, you'll have to report it, won't you? If you want my evidence, we can think up some way of presenting it without making my presence here seem suspicious — '

'Leave it to me,' she said coldly.

'It only requires a bit of thinking out. We needn't be involved — personally implicated, I mean.'

Jess opened the door.

'Will you please go?'

Andrew went out into the corridor. He had a moment of dizziness again, and pressed one hand to the back of his head. A lump had formed there, and there was a trickle of blood matting his hair. He brought his hand away sticky.

'Are you all right, old chap?'

The voice was quiet and friendly, but it struck a gasp from Jessica.

Andrew swayed round. He found

himself confronted by Western, in an olive green silk dressing gown. His hair was slightly rumpled but otherwise he looked his usual smooth, bleak self.

'I . . . I fell against a door. On my way to the lavatory.'

'Ah.'

There was something too derisively provocative in that monosyllable. Andrew burst out: 'And what the hell are you doing prowling around at this hour of the night? Taken on a job as house detective, or something?'

Western smiled thinly. 'I, too, have found it necessary to respond to a call of nature. Fortunately I avoided any collision with a door. I do hope you're all right, old chap. Can I help you back to your room?'

'No,' said Andrew. 'No. I'll manage, thank you.' He turned towards Jessica. It was essential to establish one or two facts. 'Thank you for helping me, Miss Rogers,' he said emphatically. 'I'm sorry I woke you up.'

'That's quite all right,' said Jessica.

Western nodded politely to her and

walked away, the narrow smile still on his lips.

'Damn,' said Andrew. 'Damn. That's done it. Now we'll *have* to work out some story before he spreads a nice little story of his own — '

'Leave it to me,' said Jessica again. 'Leave the whole thing to me.'

'But Western — '

'Western will not say a word,' she said coldly and confidently. 'Stay out of it, Andrew, and don't worry. Let me handle it my way.'

★   ★   ★

'Leave it to me,' said Dampier. 'I'll deal with it.'

He tried to maintain his usual blandly condescending manner, but he had been severely shaken and was sure that Jessica Rogers was not deceived.

She had told him how her suspicions about Philip Western had been aroused. He felt she was glossing over one or two details — she had been especially reticent about the circumstances of Western's

107

appearance in the corridor last night and her own reason for being awake at that time — but on the whole she was a sound, intelligent girl and not prone to jumping to hasty conclusions.

Dampier was very unhappy. He liked his job and had no wish to look for another. He enjoyed working for Intersyn and exercising his small but significant power. It was not that he worshipped his employers or paid any greater due to them than the tithe of lip service. He did not trust them and knew exactly what their much publicised concern with their workers' welfare was worth; but he had felt that so long as they appreciated the work he did for them, the propaganda he implanted in the minds of Course members and the reports he gave of those members, he was safe. If that appreciation had now soured he expected no quarter. Nothing spectacular would happen. Intersyn didn't work that way. Nobody got fired from Intersyn. There was rarely any unpleasantness. All that happened was that you were tactfully advised to look for another job, for which you would be given excellent references. If you were in a lowly position you were usually allowed six months' grace. In a senior position you might get as long as two years, though it was expected that you would have enough pride to want to remove your backside from your chair long before that time was up.

It was unthinkable that he should be eased out after he had played the Intersyn game so loyally and unflaggingly. There must be somebody behind this. There must be an element of nepotism in it somewhere. If he was to be replaced, whose was the chosen candidate?

He hated to admit to the Rogers girl that he was in any way vulnerable, but she knew a great deal already and she had been decent enough to let him in on the secret. He had to trust her and put himself in her hands. He said:

'Miss Thompson's quite unwarranted remark about the previous American course . . . and so on . . . did she say anything more? That is — ah — did she offer any more speculations, impertinent as they might be?'

Jessica hesitated.

'Come now, Miss Rogers . . . Jessica.' His joviality rang false in his own ears 'You've gone this far. You must tell me all.'

She said: 'Miss Thompson mentioned that the nomination for this Course member came from Mr Partridge.'

'Partridge. Indeed.'

Dampier felt even sadder. The plot was not merely thickening: it was becoming glutinous. There had never been a great deal of love lost between himself and Partridge, the only one of the five working Directors with whom he had never got on. Partridge and his gang of technicians always professed to look down on the London office departments. 'We make the stuff,' was one of Partridge's overworked pronouncements, 'and then you lot find ways of not selling it.' He had made it quite clear that in his opinion all time not spent on intensive research and production and on hard-selling marketing was time wasted. The subtleties of the soft sell were beyond him. Partridge's henchman, the senior chemist who gave several of the

Course lectures at Belby, consistently did his best to make life awkward for Dampier. Dampier prided himself that he passed off these conflicts successfully. By letting his class know well in advance before going to Belby that there existed a healthy rivalry between the production and marketing functions, by telling jokes against himself and even quoting Partridge's own remark with a deprecating, we-know-better-don't-we smile, he inoculated them against any barbs that might strike home. It was all, he implied, part of the Intersyn family friendly rivalry — good for the individual and good for the Company.

And now Partridge had used his influence to appoint a watcher, a spy. Partridge wanted someone else to take over Dampier's job.

But there was nobody else who could do it as well. Dampier was not himself top management material and had accepted this at an early stage of his career. He was, however, a reliable assessor of other people's merits. Those who can't, teach. Dampier could not make the grade but had an infallible instinct for detecting those who could. He would declare without false modesty that he had the qualifications of an accountant, a psychiatrist and a recruiting officer.

Some of his colleagues thought he was vain. He knew what they said behind his back — knew that he was nicknamed 'The Ferret' — and none of it harmed him. He was irreplaceable. Yet now there was a danger of a possible replacement. Perhaps he had been too complacent. His only fear had been that one day he would lose his knack and be no longer susceptible to reason or to swiftly garnered and swiftly tabulated impressions. He could not believe that this time had come. He still had the ability to coax his adult pupils into revealing their best and even more significantly their worst.

To Jessica he said: 'This is all most distressing. I do feel, though, that it may not be as sinister as it appears.'

'I'm sorry.' She reacted to the tone of his voice rather than to his actual words. 'I didn't like to say anything at first, but after last night I thought you ought to know about it.'

'Quite right. Thank you.'

'Are you going to make out an official report? I don't want to cause Miss Thompson any trouble — '

'Miss Thompson,' he declared, 'deserves all the trouble that may befall her. But' — he was cheered and in some way strengthened by the thought of that elderly, irritating spinster at his mercy — 'I don't think it advisable to take any steps at this stage. It would only hold up the Course and cause a great deal of unpleasantness.'

He could challenge Western and get the whole affair out in the open. The other Directors wouldn't approve of Partridge's methods. Partridge would not be popular. But then, neither would Dampier himself. Intersyn was not happy about having things out in the open: it was something they had always avoided. It was vulgar to make scenes, even when you were demonstrably in the right.

He said: 'I shall be obliged if you will, for the time being, keep all this to yourself. It may be possible to straighten

113

this whole deplorable business out before the Course is ended.'

'Or it may get worse,' said Jessica.

It was a comment not in the best of taste. Dampier frowned. 'Just leave it to me,' he said. 'I'll deal with Mr Western in my own way.'

6

On the Thursday evening before the Course set off for Belby, Andrew caught up with Jessica as she walked back from the Intersyn building to the hotel. She had half expected him to do so. Several times in the past few days he had tried to speak to her but she had ignored him. She had wanted to relent but was determined that she must be strong.

Now, without preamble, he said: 'Jess — what are you doing this weekend?'

'Getting ready,' she said, 'like everyone else for the trip to the barren north.'

'You're not going to visit that young idiot, are you?'

She looked straight ahead. 'What are you going to do, Andrew?' she parried.

'Look, Jess, you know we agreed — '

'By agreeing, you mean that you said what you intended to do and expected me to fall in with your wishes. All right. I'm doing just that. You're going to spend the weekend with your wife, and I am left to my own devices.'

'You know I've got to go home.'

'I know. I'm not complaining.'

'As soon as the Course is over — '

'Let's wait until we get there, shall we?' she said. 'Don't make any promises. You may not want to keep them.'

Andrew opened his mouth to continue the argument, but at that moment Hornbrook crossed the road ahead of them and stayed a few paces in front. He might be able to overhear them. It was not until they reached a road junction and traffic cut them off from Hornbrook that it was possible to resume. By now they were only a hundred yards from the hotel.

Andrew said: 'All I asked was whether you're going away to stay with young Marsh.'

It was too much. Sickeningly Jessica knew that he still had her in a firm grasp. She slowed and looked at him. His expression was cross and unloving but she wanted him as much as ever. When she hated it was herself and her undisciplined

116

emotions she hated, not Andrew.

'You know I won't,' she said wearily. 'You know I'll go to the flat and wait. I've waited so often, so long. It's a habit now. And you won't come. You won't, Andrew . . . will you?'

She gave him no chance to reply. It would have been humiliating for both of them to go over the same excuses and the same harshly rational explanations.

They reached the hotel and went in and separated.

On the Friday evening Andrew went home to his wife and Jessica went to her flat.

It was cold and unwelcoming, in some way hollow. It felt unlived in, although she had been back each weekend during the Course. It was not just that Andrew was missing: everything had seeped away, leaving the rooms empty and echoing.

And you won't come. You won't, Andrew . . . will you?

Yet still she had that wild, absurd feeling that he might. He and his wife might quarrel as soon as he got home, and at long last he would do what he had always promised to do: he would throw a few things into a bag and come here and stay here.

No; she knew he wouldn't come.

After a sleepless night she telephoned David Marsh on the Saturday morning.

'Is that invitation still open?'

'It certainly is,' he said with an eagerness that made her feel better. At the same time she felt the urge to retreat as suddenly as she had felt the urge to telephone him. Hurriedly she said: 'Just for the afternoon, I meant. I'll only come down for an hour or two. Or tomorrow, if that's more convenient.'

'No,' he said. 'Come for the weekend. We'd love to have you. How long will it take you to get ready? The trains . . . I've got a timetable somewhere here . . . '

She arrived in time for lunch. The house was smaller than she had visualised. The name of Maidenhead had conjured up in her mind a picture of large crenellated mansions with lawns sloping down towards the river. David and his widowed mother lived in a semi-detached villa below the railway embankment.

Approaching trains set up a steady thrumming as they came closer and as they passed there was a momentary pulsation right through the house.

'Quite close to the station,' said David unnecessarily.

He was wearing grey slacks and a light yellow shirt, with a green and yellow silk cravat. He looked too neat to be informal, and every now and then plucked at his cravat to make sure that it was not sagging away from his throat.

Mrs Marsh was a small woman, too bent and shrivelled for her years. There seemed to be too much weight on her shoulders. It pushed her down and she had grown tired trying to thrust herself upright. Only her eyes were still bright and lively, like David's eyes. The house, too, was bright: it was easy to see that she spent all her time dusting and polishing, plumping up cushions, scrubbing and cleaning and tidying up. Or, rather, Jessica corrected herself after a quick appraisal, that was how she spent most of her time; some must be left over for attending to the cacti. There were cacti on every window ledge and most other flat surfaces. They sprouted from pots of all shapes, all sizes. There were pots in little white-painted baskets and in plastic troughs — an Intersyn product — and in miniature gardens. There were knobbly cacti and spiky cacti, some lean and spare, some bulbous and bloated. When invited to sit down and make herself at home, Jessica could hardly resist a swift glance at her chair to make sure that some spiny object was not already in possession.

'Now, I'll just run along and get on with dinner,' said Mrs Marsh. 'It won't take long. Davy, if Miss Rogers would like a glass of sherry . . . we've got some, I think, haven't we? . . . I haven't looked properly, but I think there's some in the sideboard. Or would you like a cup of tea?'

'Can I come and help?' asked Jessica.

'No, not really. It's such a tiny kitchen. Of course, if you'd like to look . . . see round the house . . . '

It did not take long. The kitchen was indeed small and there was not room enough for two people to work comfortably in it. When the cellar door was opened it was impossible to stand at the sink. The two main bedrooms were of a reasonable size but congested with heavy furniture. The small room over the hall, in which Jessica was to sleep, had space for a single bed, a chair, and a diminutive chest of drawers. Everything was clean; and everything was faded. Within a few years the patterns on carpets and curtains and bed covers might all be bleached away to a uniform greyness.

'And now you go and sit down,' said Mrs Marsh as they came downstairs again. 'Davy will keep you company. I expect you've got a lot to talk about. Your job, I mean,' she added hastily. 'It must all be so interesting. You must tell me about it. Davy tells me such a lot, of course. But there must be a lot more to tell.'

When they were alone together there was a long pause. Jessica wondered if she had been wise to come. It showed every sign of being a stiff, awkward weekend. They would make shy conversation and there would be long gaps; and she noticed now that there were no ashtrays, remembered that she had never seen David smoking, and thought it most likely that Mrs Marsh didn't like cigarette smoke in her aseptic sitting room.

David cleared his throat and said: 'Oh — do you smoke? I'm afraid I haven't got any cigarettes, but — '

'It's quite all right.'

'No, really. Do smoke.' He looked round the room. She had a vision of tapping ash behind one of the larger cacti. 'We've got an ashtray somewhere. My father used to smoke a pipe.'

He went out of the room. She supposed that his father was the man whose framed photograph dominated the mantelpiece, framed by two cacti which appeared to be cloaked in cobwebs — an unlikely phenomenon in this house.

When they sat down to lunch and she was facing in a different direction, she saw another picture of the same man, this time standing beside Mrs Marsh, with a small boy squatting on the ground before them.

'My husband,' said Mrs Marsh abruptly. 'He was a great man.'

David reached out and put his hand on hers. Mrs Marsh squeezed it gratefully but went on looking at Jessica as though challenging her.

Jessica said: 'He worked for Intersyn too, didn't he?'

'Jessica knows everything about everybody in the firm,' said David. 'It's frightening.'

'Frightening. Yes, it must be.' Mrs Marsh seemed to shrink even further, huddled up in her chair so that she looked positively baleful. 'Dreadful people,' she burst out.

'Mother — '

'My husband's whole life was given to your firm,' Mrs Marsh went on, her eyes brighter than ever. 'He never got his just reward. Nor did we. Davy knows that. But Davy will make up for it. Davy's going to put everything right, aren't you, dear?'

'Yes,' said David soothingly.

He started to talk about films and about two recent books he had read.

Jessica had seen one of the films and gave the right answers, keeping the flow of conversation moving away from Intersyn. Mrs Marsh looked puzzled, then the light in her eyes faded and she listened apathetically for a while before ceasing to listen altogether.

After lunch David suggested a run in the car. It was the first time he had mentioned a car. When Jessica looked surprised he said: 'I don't bring it up to London. Hopeless driving in Town — and it certainly wouldn't be any good on the Course.'

'You two go,' said Mrs Marsh.

'A little trip along the river — '

'Not today. You don't want me.' Before there could be any argument Mrs Marsh headed for the stairs. 'Go off and enjoy yourselves. I'm going to lie down.'

They drove out of the town along a road that curled in towards the river and looked down on it for a while before losing itself in the trees. A convoy of swans flickered white; two girls with a crackling transistor radio shrieked at the swans and turned white-masked faces towards the road as David drove past.

He said: 'I hope it doesn't worry you. My mother talking so much about my father, I mean. He still means everything to her.'

He displayed no resentment. He was stating a simple, comprehensible fact.

Jessica wanted him to stop and put his arm round her. She wanted something to happen — anything to shake up the pattern of her life. David was young, untarnished; but he had been shut away for too long. Seeing his home and his mother, she was beginning to understand more about him than could ever be gathered from those detailed, soulless dossiers which Intersyn kept so religiously. There was an inner tension in him that, released, could be exciting. He had a lot to learn but he would learn quickly. She wondered if she could be his teacher, drawing him out from the oppression of his father's shadow.

As though in answer to her thoughts he said: 'I wish I'd met you sooner.'

'Sooner?' she laughed.

'It would have made all the difference.'

'You sound like an old man,' she said, still laughing uneasily. 'So disillusioned.'

'I've got reason.'

She did not know whether he was talking of his personal life or of the firm. It was too soon to probe. If he wanted to tell her, he would tell her.

But she said: 'It's never too late.' A comfortable generalisation, to be taken any way you wanted to take it. 'Never too late,' she repeated. 'Is it?'

'I don't know. I wish I did.'

They had reached a lock. The afternoon was cool but the sunshine had lured a number of young people out, chattering at the water's edge as they waited for a boat to negotiate the lock.

'We'd better turn back,' said David. 'Mum will be expecting us in for tea.'

At tea-time Mrs Marsh made a conscientious effort to play the hostess. She asked what Jessica thought of their town and of the river. She listened politely and made an unexpected joke about the young men in sports cars who drove in on Saturday evenings. Then she said: 'When Mr Marsh and I first came to live here . . . ' And her face darkened, and after that her politeness was only a formality, maintained with difficulty. At every possible opportunity she introduced the name — 'Mr Marsh' this, and 'Mr Marsh' that. Jessica was aware that David was watching her closely as though afraid that she would go too far.

It was not until the middle of the evening that a small outburst came.

'The lies they told,' she said, apropos of nothing that had gone before. 'All those terrible lies about negligence — not a word of truth in it.'

'Now, Mother, please — '

'They want to stop us finding out,' she said. 'They'll do anything to stop us finding out. But they won't, will they, Davy?'

'We'll sort it all out,' he said soothingly.

'He's a good boy,' said Mrs Marsh to Jessica. It was a fierce statement, almost an order. 'He's been a good boy to me. You'll help him, won't you?'

'Of course,' said Jessica uncomfortably.

When David saw her up to her room he apologised again. 'I didn't know she'd carry on like that. I told her not to talk about . . . about the past.'

'I didn't quite understand. She seems to have some idea that — '

'It's nothing,' he said. But his eyes were so like his mother's that the disclaimer did not ring true. 'I'll tell you all about it one day.'

That 'one day' introduced a new note. She realised as he spoke how funny it was — funny, and rather sweet — that he should have seen her to her room this way, as though his home were a mansion with long, misleading corridors instead of this compact semi-detached house.

Again it was funny, and again rather sweet, when he put one hand awkwardly on her shoulder and kissed her.

'Good night, Jessica.'

His mouth was clean and fresh. This was a pleasant, undemanding good night kiss. When she had gone to bed and the sounds of David and his mother coming to their rooms and going to bed had ceased, she lay awake and tried to decide whether it was the prelude to something more important and whether that was what she wanted it to be. She tried to debate the matter rationally with herself, but found that her eyelids were closing. Her thoughts tripped over one another, leaving behind ragged edges which curled up into new, grotesque shapes. Last night she had not slept. Tonight she was asleep before she knew what had happened, before she had even accustomed herself to being in a strange bed in a strange house. When she awoke it was morning.

She felt in a strangely carefree mood as though she were on holiday. Somehow things could be simple and delightful from now on — if that was how she wanted them to be.

David, too, had relaxed. He was not so anxiously polite. He behaved towards her as though she were often here, so that there was no need to make a special effort on her behalf. Mrs Marsh was very quiet; perhaps he had spoken to her. Jessica was conscious of a flicker of disquiet: there was something here that she was sure she ought to know. But she did not want the day spoilt and she put the vague questions out of her mind.

Only once was the day's equilibrium disturbed. After lunch Mrs Marsh cleared away and Jessica went out into the kitchen with her. It was now accepted that she could help with the washing-up. As she was drying plates and putting them on the table immediately behind her, squeezing past Mrs Marsh in the confined space, Mrs Marsh asked her the usual obvious questions about where she lived — 'On your own, in London?' — and where her parents lived — 'Fancy being that far away, oh, I wouldn't like that.' And then out of the blue she said sharply: 'Davy's got a lot to do before he thinks of getting married.' It was a warning.

'I'm sure he has,' was all that Jessica could say.

The remark stayed with her during the early part of the afternoon but gradually David's unforced cheerfulness washed it away. It only came back with full force when Jessica looked at her watch and said that she would like to go back home reasonably early. To her surprise he said:

'I wouldn't mind coming back with you.'

'But you don't have to be in all that early in the morning.'

'A lot of them will be back in the hotel tonight.'

'Only if they have a long journey.'

'I wouldn't mind. I could see you home.'

'I know the way, thank you, David. Besides' — she meant there to be laughter in it but it came out oddly hard — 'it would give your mother quite the wrong ideas.'

He laughed in reply, and his laugh, too, was unreal. 'In that case I could come up by a later train.'

She was taken aback. Suddenly she resented Mrs Marsh's threat, and she heard herself say, 'Well, if you're proposing to follow me, I can always provide you with a divan in the sitting room.'

He let out a strange little sigh. He might almost have been waiting for this invitation, leading up to it.

'It would be nicer than the hotel,' he said.

She was not sure that she had expected to be taken up so promptly. Perhaps it would all go wrong now. She was rushing things without even knowing if she wanted them to happen at all.

David was disconcertingly calm. When they got back to the house he told his mother without a trace of self-consciousness that Jessica was going back by an early train and that he would go along later to the hotel. 'Don't want the long-distance men to put in too much work this evening and get a lead on me,' he said easily. There was a silence in which Mrs Marsh digested this. Jessica waited apprehensively.

'Well,' said Mrs Marsh after a minute of rumination, 'if you're going up to London tonight anyway, the least you can do is see Miss Rogers home.'

Jessica said, 'I'm quite used to — '

'Silly for you to go up separately. Doesn't make sense.'

All at once they were hurrying to get ready. In the dusk they were on their way towards London. They said little in the train.

David's shyness returned when he was shown into the flat. He walked carefully as though afraid of tripping over something. When she left him in the sitting room while she went out to make coffee, he remained standing. When she came back and indicated a chair, he lowered himself gingerly into it and kept his hands tightly clenched on his knees.

'That's a nice picture,' he said tentatively.

It was a water colour of the Malverns, bought because she and Andrew had spent a weekend there early on in their relationship when everything was flawless.

'My favourite,' she said, 'is the one behind you.'

He dutifully slewed round in his chair and studied scarlet fruit and black shadows of the picture she had found three months ago and loved at first sight. He sat in that twisted position for quite a time, obviously trying to find something to say.

'Coffee . . . ?'

He turned thankfully back to her. 'Oh, thanks. Yes. Lovely.'

'Black or white?'

'Er, white. No. Black.' Then he nodded

towards the far wall and said brusquely: 'That's the divan.'

'That's it.' She poured coffee into his cup and passed it along the low, oiled teak table to him.

The room overawed him. It was not much larger than the sitting room of his home but Jessica had aimed at airiness and achieved it, and its whole atmosphere was so different that he was lost. She didn't want him to feel lost: she wanted them both to be at ease, discovering each other without strain and enjoying the discovery as they had done earlier today.

David said: 'When did you join Intersyn?'

This wouldn't do at all. Before they knew where they were they would be halfway back into the Course, with the implicit chalking up of marks. She was not ready to slip into her rôle of an Intersyn employee this evening. She didn't want to talk about her career, and she had no intention of asking him about his. She knew about his.

That was the trouble. Caught up in

Intersyn, she knew too much about most of the men she met. Few of them came from outside the Company. It was too easy to check the records of those she met inside. One of her girl-friends in Staff Records had once said: 'Any time a man asks me out to dinner I dash off to see if he has a wife and six kids and if his salary is high enough for him to buy me the sort of food I want to eat.' Even if you didn't work it out in terms of progeny and restaurants, it was difficult not to know too much about the men you met inside Intersyn. And men outside were just that: men outside. After a while you found that the Company had engulfed you. You derided its standards yet implicitly accepted them. People outside just didn't understand. You found that you had few topics of mutual interest.

But not now. Not tonight.

She said: 'You don't have to sit so far away.'

There was nothing accomplished or calculated in his movements. He came towards her in a hurry as though scared that if his first impetus failed he wouldn't be able to go through with it. When he bent over her to kiss her he lost his balance and fell on top of her; and then they were laughing and couldn't stop, and Jessica put her arms round him and held him down so that he couldn't get up, and bit his ear. His foot kicked the edge of the table. The coffee cups rattled. His hands were unskilled.

'No,' she gasped. 'No . . . not here.'

When they reached the bedroom she was afraid he was going to make an inventory of its contents. She caught his arm and pulled him close to her more vigorously than she had intended. He fumbled with her blouse; it was funny and sweet and they began to laugh again, but his laughter was breathless and uncertain. He was not used to this. He was afraid that it might all go wrong.

Jessica unfastened her blouse quickly and slipped it off. Her fingers were on the zip of her skirt when the telephone at her bedside rang.

David, about to take off his tie with slightly trembling hands, froze.

The telephone went insistently on.

Jessica fell back on the bed and reached for the receiver.

Andrew said: 'I've been trying to get you all afternoon.'

'I've been away for the weekend,' she said lightly, smiling up at David so that he should see this was not an important call.

'Oh. So you went.'

'Yes. Had a nice time?'

'Jess . . . ' He could not suppress the annoyance but was trying hard. 'I could get away. I could start out now.'

'Oh, I wouldn't if I were you.'

David was slowly taking off his tie, ready to put it back on again if the alarm was given.

'A lot of them will be getting back to the hotel tonight,' said Andrew. 'I could come back. I've already told Muriel that it's really the best policy. It's convincing enough.'

She smiled. He could not see her smile, and he would not have understood. Really, Andrew was too consistently Andrew. It meant a lot to him that there should be a rational excuse — one which fitted the circumstances, which could indeed be as near true as made no difference. He could just as well have used it if it had been untrue, but he would not have been easy in his mind.

'I don't think so,' she said casually.

'Are you alone?'

Her mind raced. But there was only one possible answer. She said simply: 'No.'

Andrew rang off.

'Anything important?' said David.

'No.'

She drew him down upon her. When she saw the anxiety in his face, she reached for the light switch and snapped it off. Then it was better; better for him, better for both of them.

He was awkward and unsatisfying and did not know that he was not satisfying her. But she felt a rush of tenderness towards him and when it was ended she ran her hand rhythmically, contentedly down his back.

It was only when he was asleep and she lay still awake that the echoes of Andrew's voice began to throb through the room. She could half pretend that it was Andrew who lay beside her, his head burrowed into her shoulder — but only half pretend, for Andrew liked to move away to the edge of the bed, and there was a different feeling, a different smell about him. She was suddenly frightened — not of Andrew melodramatically appearing here now and making a scene, but of Andrew never appearing here again.

At the same time she wanted to be free of him. Her hand moved over David's shoulder and down his smooth arm to the elbow.

He murmured in his sleep and instinctively moved away from her.

It happened too often. The movement away — in bed, in the street, in her whole relationship with Andrew there had been this moving away. She held on to David, and he groaned and was awake. Like Andrew he came awake quickly.

She didn't want another Andrew. Whatever she wanted, it was not that.

They lay there for some minutes. Her hand caressed his arm until he twitched beneath her and she knew that he wanted her to stop. He was staring up at the ceiling. She could see only the faint outline of his head, but there was a glimmer of light on his eyes. She lay back beside him. We're like two noble corpses, she thought waywardly, on a marble tomb: two of us, flat on our backs, staring sightlessly at the sky or the ceiling or whatever.

He said: 'Jessica.'

'Mm?'

'Who's watching me? Who's been told off to watch me on the Course?'

7

The trip to the North had an aura of adventure about it. Although the name of Belby was frequently on the lips of Head Office staff and visitors from overseas marketing companies, few of the Course members had ever been there. It was remote and rather frightening, almost mythical. They felt as though they were heading for the Siberian salt mines as privileged spectators — spectators about to be faced by some of the unpleasant realities behind their daily food and warmth.

For some the journey itself was not too remarkable. Those who lived in the North or Midlands had the advantage of a longer Monday morning tacked on to their weekend: they made their own way from their homes to Belby and the Company hostel on the edge of the plant, meeting the London contingent in the late afternoon.

Andrew, making his way along the train in search of a vacant seat, found himself at the door of a first-class compartment which so far contained Dampier, Hornbrook and Western. He hesitated. It would surely seem rather ostentatious to join Dampier. He didn't want it to look as though he were trying to steal a march or ingratiate himself. Then it occurred to him that neither Hornbrook nor Western had hesitated or would ever hesitate in such circumstances. They took it as their due that they should sit with Dampier.

Andrew went in and joined them.

Just before the train drew out two other Course members arrived. Startled by their own temerity, they sat down and remained silent for the larger part of the journey.

Hornbrook talked affably to Dampier about various aspects of Company operations. What he said bore little relation to the techniques they were studying on the Course yet casually a picture was built up of Hornbrook as a man steeped in all the workings of the Company and its associates here and abroad. He even achieved an air of condescension towards Dampier. The lecturer might be the man of power during these few weeks but Hornbrook would go far beyond him in the future. Hornbrook was like a junior officer in training: he had to defer to the regimental sergeant major for the time being but the time was not far distant when he would be in a position of authority which the sergeant major could never attain.

Andrew answered when politely drawn into the conversation by Dampier but felt churlishly reluctant to contribute anything of his own. He thought mainly about Jessica and about his weekend at home.

Muriel had been pettish. He hadn't done much to overcome her mood. He hadn't wanted to. It was almost a satisfaction that she should be so spiteful. She was not even in the house when he got home. He had put the key in the door and tensed, waiting for the imminent meeting, already braced against the offhandedly contemptuous welcome at which she was so adept; and then there had been the deflation when he found the place empty. Typical that she should be out. She knew what time he was due back so there was no likelihood of a misunderstanding. It was deliberate.

It was an hour before she appeared. When she came in, tossing her coat across the back of a chair, all she said was:

'Oh, hello.'

'Hello. I wondered where you were.'

'Playing bridge. You know I always go to Dulcie's on a Friday afternoon.'

'You're not usually as late as this.'

'I didn't know you ever noticed whether I was late or not.'

It was not worth his while to say that he had expected her to be here to meet him. After all, she was the one who had made the fuss about his going away and about his coming home for only one weekend after leaving her on her own all that time, so she was the one who ought to have been eager for their reunion. But logic had nothing to do with Muriel's actions. If he asked her now why she hadn't been here to greet him she would ask with sour delight if he had really missed her, and say between her teeth that she was touched, really touched. There was really nothing to be said. But since they could hardly sit or stand in silence he would have to speak, and he sensed already that whatever he said would trigger off some prepared sneer. She was primed, ready to react to whatever line he took.

Andrew opened his brief-case and said: 'I brought you this.'

It was a bottle of scent. He had been driven to buy it by some obscure feeling that he was coming back from holiday and that he ought to buy a present for the neglected little woman back home. On this at any rate Muriel was in agreement with him.

'Anyone would think you'd been to France,' she said.

He held out the bottle. She took it. Then she said:

'I gave up using this scent ages ago.'

'You've been using it recently. That's why I — '

'You wouldn't notice, of course. Ages ago.'

'You can always go back to it,' said

Andrew. 'You used to be fond enough of it.'

Muriel shrugged and put the bottle down on the coffee table. Indifferently she said:

'Smuggle anything else through the Customs?'

He took out a half-bottle of Tia Maria. It had always been her favourite drink.

'Don't tell me you've gone off this as well?' He tried to make his tone of voice as much a peace offering as the two bottles had been. She at once felt that she had got him on the run, and said:

'You must have a guilty conscience about something, Andrew.'

He was a stranger in his own home. He couldn't imagine why he was here or what pleasure there would ever be here. He stuck it out until the middle of Sunday afternoon — the greater part of two purposeless, graceless days — and then said that he thought he would go back into town late that afternoon instead of getting up for the early train in the morning. 'Mustn't let any of them steal a march on me' — it was too contrived a remark and was received sceptically. It gave Muriel an excuse to shut herself away in a hurt, defeated silence. He suggested they should go out for a walk. She said that he could go for a walk on his own. He went, and from a telephone box tried to ring Jessica. There was no answer. Later, back in the house, he tried again, having first made sure that Muriel was settled for a spell in the bathroom. Still there was no reply. He fretted until the pub down the road opened and he could plausibly say he was going out for a quick pint. He asked Muriel to come with him but did so in just such a way that he could guarantee her refusing. This time he spoke to Jessica and she made it clear that she had somebody with her.

He remembered all too clearly the telephone beside her bed. She had answered it quickly. She must have been in the bedroom. That did not necessarily mean that David Marsh was in the bedroom with her . . .

The train rattled across points and set up a frenzy of echoes in a small station as it screamed through. There was nothing to do in the train but think. Impossible to read and impossible to join in the complacent conversation. He was a stranger in his home, a stranger in Jess's flat, a stranger here in this compartment with these strangers and enemies. He was on his own. All right, let it be that way

Even as he made this silent proclamation he found himself nevertheless saying to Western, 'Is there a buffet car on this train?'

'Thirsty?' said Western as though inviting Dampier to make a note in the records that Andrew Flint was an incipient alcoholic.

Andrew went out of the compartment and along the corridor. In the noisy, unstable space between two carriages he rubbed shoulders with David Marsh. The train swayed and they were jostled together. Andrew caught Marsh's arm, and instinctively his grip tightened. He found himself reaching out with his free hand, gripping Marsh with that, too.

'Hey, careful . . . '

There was a smell of dust and grease, and from under their feet the noise was a physical battering. David Marsh, twisting away towards the brighter daylight of the corridor, looked scared. Andrew couldn't let go. He wanted to shake the kid, frighten him, yell some sense into him and then toss him aside and never see him again.

Suddenly Western edged into the constricted space.

'Thought I might join you.'

Andrew let go of Marsh, and the young man moved apprehensively away. Western watched him go.

'Bad marks against candidates who try to throttle their rivals, old boy,' he said as he followed Andrew towards the buffet car. 'Sign of insecurity.'

When they reached the car and settled at a small white-topped table it was Western who did most of the talking. He was quite at ease. He discussed their fellow Course members, made a joke about Dampier that was shrewd yet inoffensive if it should ever get back to Dampier, and implicitly invited Andrew to contribute an opinion of his own.

Then, after they had ordered coffee, he

brought Jessica's name into the conversation.

'Very ornamental. But functional also. She could probably assess us just as efficiently as Dampier's likely to. Even before the Course started she probably knew as much about us as anyone possibly could. Don't you think so?'

'I wouldn't be surprised,' said Andrew stiffly.

He wondered if Western was part of the whole complex Company espionage system. Industrial career development, like the operation of a spy ring, fed on itself and put forth shoots that tangled inextricably with one another.

Only cowards were afraid of this monster and its tentacles. Andrew felt a resurgence of energy and determination, provoked by Western's slyness. You could always cut your way through that sort of thing. If the weak went down, that was their lookout. You could always win a duel with the psychological aptitude tests, defy the concealed microphones and the studiously casual listener; and while the management selection boys were thinking up new trials and oppressions you could be thinking up ways of circumventing them. It was a matter of being constantly alert, flexible in manoeuvre. And wasn't that what business had always demanded? The only difference was that in the old days you had had to out-think your competitors, while today the first essential was to out-think your colleagues.

Suddenly he felt so sure of himself that when he was ready to go back to his compartment he did not even bother to wait for Western to finish his coffee. He got up confidently and went back on his own, seeing Western's head jerk back in mild surprise.

On the way back he looked down through the glass pane into a compartment where Jessica was sitting. All the seats were occupied. She looked up, caught his eye, and looked away.

The bitch. He wanted her. He couldn't have lost her to a kid like Marsh. It would be all right later when this was all over.

Later. But he wanted her now.

Jessica turned back in time to see Andrew swaying along the corridor, letting his shoulders take the impact on each side. A few minutes later Western went past.

In her mind grew a larger and larger question mark after Western's name. For him the results of the Course were a foregone conclusion. He was already established. He was already a management man. His only task was to establish the unworthiness of another man.

Another man — Dampier or David Marsh?

Jessica could not resolve this. As the train thrummed on its way she put her head back against the creased linen rest attached to the seat and closed her eyes. Beside her two men muttered a conversation. Beyond them, far away but clear, the remembered voice of David asked her the utterly unexpected question.

Who's been told off to watch me on the Course?

It had been such a plaintive plea. He had had to repeat it before she could grasp what he had said. Then she had not at first taken it seriously. There was no reason why anyone should watch David

Marsh. He was not big enough; not important enough to anyone.

'Whatever makes you think . . . ?'

'There is somebody.' He was so sure. 'Going through things in my room, checking on me, watching.'

'But why should they?'

'Because they're afraid of what I might know. Or what I might suspect. I've got closer than they meant me to: it must be worrying one or two of them.'

'What could you suspect? I mean — David, what have you got on your mind?'

It was not what she had expected or wanted, this abrupt switch from things that were personal and special to the dreary world of the Executive Course. She didn't know what he was talking about and didn't much want to know.

'I'll tell you one day.' He exuded a strange confidence, somehow establishing the fact that what happened from now on was under his control rather than hers. His hand brushed her hip and lingered. She hoped they would go back to being what they had been and say nothing more about Intersyn and its real or imagined threats. But David went on: 'You know all about the people on this Course, Jessica. If anyone can tell me, you can. Who's watching?'

She could have told him. But she did not believe. It might do a lot of damage to tell him about Western and put him on a false trail. There was no reason why a man of Partridge's standing, a Director, should have gone to such lengths to appoint Western specially to keep an eye on David Marsh.

'You're imagining things,' she said.

'No.'

'It tells on your nerves, the whole atmosphere. I know that. But it's *meant* to. That's the whole idea. It keeps you on your mettle. I know Dampier's little tricks — and you'll find it's just the same at Belby. They all want to turn you inside out. I'm not surprised you've got this feeling of being watched. You're all being watched, all the time. That's what the Course is for.'

'No,' he insisted, 'I'm being personally spied on. Is that part of the Course?'

Jess tried to answer, but was too drowsy

to do more than mumble. Sleep came up from inside her, thickening her tongue and jumbling the words in her mind into ludicrous patterns.

'You're not going to tell me,' said David. 'You know, but you're not going to tell me.'

He sounded like a little boy. She seemed to hear him calling after her, a child unjustly abandoned, as she slid down into a simmering of dream and darkness.

Jessica started. A train slammed past, going at speed in the opposite direction. She was trapped for a moment between today and yesterday. Then she opened her eyes, yawned, and returned the timid smile offered to her by the man sitting opposite.

★　★　★

The week at Belby began vigorously. The Course members were allowed to sit down for the first half hour only and then were taken on a brief tour of the plant. This would be followed by longer and more arduous periods in each section of the plant.

'This,' said Dr Schroeder in his introductory talk, 'is the good solid cake on which Mr Dampier and his London colleagues put their pretty icing.'

Dampier smiled knowingly at his class to show that this was the time for them to recognise how right he had been. He had told them it would be like this. And he smiled at Schroeder to show that he appreciated the gibe and had been expecting it and would get his own back in due course.

Dr Schroeder was a large man with a puffy white face and wisps of grey hair sprouting around a pink-rimmed tonsure. There was a flabby heaviness in his movements but no flabbiness in his mind. He was a specialist and a fanatic. Everything that was not essential to his purpose had been fined away. He had a spare, bony mind in a pulpy body.

Some of the men tried to look at home in the middle of bristling technicalities. Others had no need for pretence. Crowther's pipe emitted smug curls of smoke: he had started his career in this part of the world, in this factory before it was modernised, and he knew what was made here and how it was made. Schroeder's terse descriptions of the various processes held no terrors for Crowther. He knew the pattern and could follow the reasoning like a pianist confronted by a piece of music which his mind has forgotten but which his fingers remember. Crowther even knew some of the workmen, still here from his time. When they nodded at him as he passed it might have been felt by other Course members that he had won an unfair advantage simply by being born in this neighbourhood. It would be different when they got back to London.

Schroeder was a high priest and this sprawling factory was to him the shrine of his religion. Apostles might go out to the ends of the earth to spread the news and sell the factory's products, but this was the meaningful reality. In some departments he described the processes with the aid of a flow chart, showing every development from the basic feedstock to the luxuriant output of innumerable plastics, synthetics and volatile gases — and his flow chart was to him a precious illuminated manuscript. In other places he would jot down in a matter of seconds long formulae on a piece of paper and pass it round, inviting their reverence.

At intervals Dampier would interject some facetious remark just to show that he was still a person of some consequence — and, moreover, a person who had heard all this before and was blandly unimpressed by it. Schroeder's answer was a fat-lipped pout of a smile and a sorrowful shake of the head which tried to be humorous but failed.

They marched inexorably through a world of polymers, of thermoplastic resins and thermosetting resins. They nodded as wisely as possible over explanations of the distinctions between the alkyd and epoxide groups, and tried to show keen yet dignified enthusiasm when Schroeder wiped his right eye with the corner of his handkerchief and grew lyrical over recent developments in cellulosics. He guided them through each process as though inventing it under their very eyes.

'And this' — obviously planned as the climax of their exhausting peregrination — 'is our unique process.' Schroeder held open a door and ushered them through into the ultimate sanctuary. 'This is the development on which Intersyn has founded over fifty per cent of its current production.'

'Syndex,' nodded Crowther. 'Biggest selling line we've got. Gives us a lead over our rivals that they're killing themselves to reduce.'

Schroeder looked hurt.

'Dr Schroeder isn't interested in the commercial aspects of the work here,' said Dampier silkily.

The two men smiled formally at each other. Schroeder waited as though well aware of what Dampier was leading up to.

'And speaking of rivals' — Dampier gave a gentle little cough that turned into a chuckle — 'I sometimes think Dr Schroeder is like those atomic scientists who want to share their secrets with the whole world instead of limiting them to one country . . . or one firm.'

He hesitated, as though to give Schroeder the chance of appealing for mercy. But Schroeder merely nodded and waited. They were going through motions they must have gone through many times before.

'Once upon a time,' Dampier proceeded, 'our Print and Paper Department designed a brochure showing how Belby functioned. It featured a splendid photograph of Dr Schroeder beside a blackboard, lecturing to visiting executives just as he is lecturing you now. The picture was vetted and approved by every technical department and pretty well every senior member of staff in Belby here. And it was not until the block had been made and proofs passed that one of our ignorant London staff just happened to notice that the equation on the blackboard in the picture was one of our most cherished top-secret formulae.'

There was an appreciative murmur. Schroeder bowed his head.

'I'm afraid,' said Dampier, 'that these technicians are so completely wrapped up in their work that they leave documents lying around, lose the keys to their cupboards, and as good as invite the enemy to come in and have a look round.'

'The enemy?' Schroeder protested mildly. 'We are not at war, Mr Dampier.'

'Aren't we?' Dampier was loud and emphatic. 'But I say that we are. To everyone on this Course I say it: we are at war. A commercial war, but as bitter and unrelenting as any other. We must fight for commercial survival.' It was impossible to tell whether this routine had been deliberately worked out between the two of them as an integral part of the Course. 'And there is espionage in this war, just as in any other.' The calculated mockery came back into Dampier's manner. 'It worries me sometimes to think how easy it would be to take every important document out of this place.'

Schroeder said: 'Our security precautions — '

'Are a disgrace. I know that *I* could crack any safe and find anything I wanted. And I'm not the only one. A complete stranger could do it, properly briefed.'

'Who would give a stranger such a briefing?'

'I don't know. But in time of war you must suspect everyone . . . and protect your secrets against everyone.'

'Perhaps,' said Schroeder, 'we may now study the operation of the plant.'

They walked in a religious hush across the gently throbbing floor of the building. It had once been a large warehouse and had then been converted piecemeal into a small refining unit. Now only the shell remained. Inside were new machines and new dials. Only two operatives were visible — and they needed to come in only every thirty minutes. Gauges in the main control room twenty yards away showed exactly what was going on in every part of the plant. The days of thundering machinery and sweating men were gone. The enclosed pipes and vessels were silent save for a faint pulsation which was felt rather than heard.

Schroeder explained the successive stages of the operation. His pupils found it hard to envisage the chemical and physical mutations taking place beneath the placidly shining surfaces. The product itself did not show up until the last minute at the far end of the extrusion and moulding shed.

'And to get the best view of it,' said Dr Schroeder, 'we will study it from above.'

Dampier smartly anticipated him by leading the way to a flight of iron steps. These went up the side of the building and levelled off along the wall at a height of about twenty feet. At the far end was a row of office windows. Dampier waved at the nearest window.

'Dr Schroeder's eyrie,' he announced. 'A wonderful vantage point. Dr Schroeder spends happy hours at his window, admiring the view.'

'This old catwalk still here,' marvelled Crowther.

'Not the old one,' said Dampier. 'It has been raised a few feet and strengthened.'

They went up in single file. Crowther tapped his knuckles against the wall to establish his long-standing acquaintance-ship with the place.

They lined up along the rail. Below them, extruded filaments like gleaming toffee were coming off rollers and blending into a sheet which then poured down a wide shute. It was like a swathe of lava but so smooth that there was no perceptible movement.

Schroeder explained. A thermosetting resin passed through stages during which specified additives were used to give it bulk and certain strengthening properties. The balance of these additives conditioned the end product, and every manufacturer strove to find the ideal combination. At a chosen temperature — again a tricky point — the synthetic resin could be moulded as required; but once set, it could not be reshaped by further heat treatment. Intersyn had developed a sequence of additives and temperature control which resulted in the toughest yet lightest plastic yet known. It could not be chipped or broken. A diamond could not even scratch the surface. No shock could fragment it; no drill could bite into it. It was resistant to atomic radiation. Already it was being used in rockets and space projectiles. Delicate instruments embedded in it could never be shattered or disturbed.

'When we finally reach the moon,' said Dampier, conveying some of the practical side of the matter to his pupils before they fell too much under the spell of the idealistic, abstracted Dr Schroeder, 'Intersyn will have made it possible.'

Schroeder winced at this further exhibition of sordid materialism.

David Marsh said: 'When was this process developed?'

'It took a considerable time,' said Schroeder. 'A great many of us worked on it.'

'Yes. But when was the final discovery made?'

Schroeder frowned reproachfully. 'In such things, there is rarely a final discovery. No genius stumbles across the answer — there are no flashes of inspiration.'

'But somebody hits on the key equation. Somebody is ahead of his colleagues, even if he doesn't always get the credit from it.'

Heads turned curiously towards him.

'You may put it that way. In this case

Mr Partridge, who is now one of our Directors, of course, assembled all the final material. It was he who formulated the basic approach, if I may express it. But Mr Partridge would be the first to admit that many others had contributed to his success. Many people worked on the project.'

'Including my father,' said David Marsh.

Schroeder looked at him. Then he nodded slowly. 'Your father? Yes, I see it.' He smiled with genuine pleasure. 'You are Richard Marsh's son. He was a very gifted man. Such a pity that he did not live to see his researches bear fruit.'

'But he did.'

'No,' said Schroeder regretfully. 'We were still in the dark when your father . . . had his accident.' He looked away; looked down into the shining, dun-coloured river below with a reminiscent smile. 'Your father and his little black notebook — always scribbling, always working harder than any of us. He was so very anxious to beat us past the post!'

'That notebook disappeared,' said David Marsh.

166

'Disappeared?'

'We never found it. It wasn't at home among his belongings, and when we asked about it here we were told it was nowhere to be found. That was the story, anyway.'

Dampier cleared his throat and prepared to intervene. But Schroeder was ahead of him — suddenly chill and in no pleasantly reminiscent mood. 'I do not understand. What are you trying to say?'

'Just that he always had his notebook with him — '

'Indeed, that is true. He would not be parted from it. So?'

'So,' said young Marsh, 'it's odd that when he died it had disappeared.'

'I do not understand,' said Schroeder again.

Before Dampier could make another attempt to regain control, Western was saying: 'I think we all accept the fact that the Company is a corporate body. We're all part of it, and we all contribute what we can. Anything we make belongs to the Company. Whether we're on the research side or on production — even out in the field, selling — we don't expect individual kudos. It's the team that counts, not the individual.' He turned abruptly towards Dampier. 'Isn't that right, Mr Dampier?'

'Absolutely.' Dampier was mutely furious that the initiative should have been plucked from him in this way. 'The team,' he said with a snap at the end of the word. 'The team, not the individual.'

He stared at Western. Some of the others who had been watching him looked uneasily away. Schroeder pushed himself back from the rail and said:

'I think it is time we moved on. There are many things we still have to see.'

Their feet shuffled echoingly along the ironwork until they came to the row of offices. They went through in groups of two or three. David Marsh was somehow, seemingly without deliberation on anyone's part, on his own. Andrew Flint and Philip Western brought up the rear, a few yards behind him.

Western said: 'A disturbing influence, that young man.'

'He's not the only one around here.' The reply was sharp and uncompromising.

Western raised his eyebrows and appeared pleased rather than curious about this remark.

★ ★ ★

Most of the following day was spent in the research laboratories. Another lecturer took over to discuss his specialised work, but Dampier was always in attendance. He watched. He studied those who made notes and those who listened. Later there would be ways of finding out which of the listeners had in fact been soaking up knowledge without any need to take notes, and which had settled into an unhappy trance.

Jessica had little to do at this stage of the Course. She could usually rely on this one day as a time for renewing old contacts, checking with the administration office that they were satisfied with the Head Office communications routine, and putting Dampier's collection of confidential notes and scribbles into some kind of order.

Late in the afternoon an envelope arrived containing a revised timetable for the rest of the week. It had been written out by Dr Schroeder. If it was to come into operation it would mean that Jess would have to type copies and circulate them to all the Course members this evening. She telephoned Schroeder's office to ask if he had really agreed this with Dampier and whether in fact the new arrangements would work: this was the first time there had been any departure from the set programme that she could recall. Schroeder was not in. He was Duty Chemist that night and would not be back in the plant until seven o'clock.

Jessica rang off and grimly began to type out a new programme, starting with a master copy on which she made notes that Dampier would need.

Dampier was late returning from the day's lectures. Probably he had spent an hour in the hostel bar, still assessing, looking for weariness, collecting other men's yawns and jotting down the mental notes that soon he would so fluently dictate to Jessica.

When he came into the office he looked unusually subdued. For a few moments he did not even acknowledge Jessica's existence; then he nodded, but when he spoke it was not really to her.

'That chap Western . . . '

She waited. But Dampier suddenly smiled, rubbed his hands together, and switched on his half paternal, half condescending smile.

'Well, now. What's all this, hm? An awful lot of paper around the place.'

'It's a new timetable.'

'It's a what?'

She told him. He was his old self again, alert and prickly as ever. Before she had finished he had taken the handwritten copy from her and was skimming over it, grunting and snorting every few seconds.

Finally he threw it back on to the desk.

'Dr Schroeder seems to imagine that this Course is run for his benefit rather than ours.'

'I've never known it altered like this

before,' she agreed.

'No need to alter it. It's always worked perfectly well, hasn't it? What are they trying to do — throw us off balance?'

Startled by his vehemence, Jessica said: 'It's probably something to do with the duty rosters for the department heads and senior chemists.'

'Damn it, they've had weeks of warning. They know when we're due here, they know what our routine is, it isn't the first time we've been here. No . . . they're just being difficult. They're playing some nasty little game. They know there isn't time to make all these readjustments — I'd have to make notes, think things out differently, alter my own lectures and summings up . . .'

This, too, was new. Jessica had rarely seen Dampier falter. He had always enjoyed the petty rivalry he encountered at Belby. Now for the first time he looked as tired as some of the Course members themselves often looked. Tired . . . and pathetically scared, with no will to fight back.

She said: 'I've done what I can. I don't

think it's as bad as it seems. It'll take me an hour or so to get the copies made, but I've already worked out your master copy and added the notes I think you'll need.'

'No!' said Dampier loudly.

'If you'll just glance over it — '

'No. I won't stand for it. If they want to know what my reaction is, they'll soon find out. If this is a test . . . '

Again he hesitated. She could almost see him working it out, narrowing his eyes and trying to see the pros and cons written out in parallel lists. As an assessor himself, how would he assess the problem with which he was now presented? To accept the alterations because a loyal employee would do so without argument and without complaint; or to reject them because the real test at this moment was one of initiative, of willingness to stand up for one's rights within the framework of efficient organisation?

Jessica picked up the timetable. Dampier took it from her once more. Then he reached for a pencil and began to scribble across the paper.

'I'm not going to be messed about by

these technical johnnies . . . Look at that, just look at it! How could we go straight from the loading bay to the distillation plant — what kind of sequence is that? — and then have a rational discussion afterwards . . . ?' He scored heavy lines until the paper tore. 'And that won't work, either. We'll put my transitional talk back where it was. And as for this . . . ' Again he was scribbling, this time at an angle, the words running round the figures on the timetable until they were nearly obscured. 'Let's see what Schroeder makes of this!'

With a flourish he handed the crumpled, ripped paper back to Jessica.

Tentatively she said: 'It's supposed to come into operation first thing in the morning. Perhaps you'd better have a word with Dr Schroeder right away. He's Duty Chemist — he should be on by now.'

Dampier glanced at his watch. A pulse twitched beneath his right eye.

'I haven't the time. You take it over to him, my dear, and present it to him with my compliments.'

'But he won't listen to me.'

'He doesn't have to listen. He can read, can't he?' Dampier could not take his eyes off the mutilated timetable. She wondered if he wanted to snatch it back, or if perhaps he would suddenly storm out of the room and go in search of Schroeder. If this had happened at any time in the past he would certainly have gone himself — and not even aggressively, but with the cool certainty that he was going to get his own way. 'No,' he said, 'I'm . . . going somewhere this evening. You'll have to do it. You'll find him easily enough. The control room will know, anyway.'

Without waiting for her to argue he turned and left the room.

Jessica again rang Schroeder's office. This time there was no reply at all. None of his staff was on duty at this time and Schroeder himself must be walking conscientiously round the plant. She smoothed and folded the timetable as well as she could, put it in her coat pocket, and went out into the cool evening.

There was still a pale lemon glow in the

western sky. Some of the metal columns and rooftops gleamed in the fading day, but between the buildings the twilight thickened.

She went to the control room and found Schroeder there, lost in contemplation of a pressure gauge.

This was the heart of the factory. Any change of temperature, pressure, viscosity, flow rate or consistency was signalled by a warning needle. A glance at the dials was enough to see exactly what was happening at any point in the hundreds of miles of pipes, twisting below and above the ground — the intestines of a huge sprawling body whose every pulse beat and alteration in breathing was recorded here. Schroeder, staring raptly at a gauge, saw beyond the finger and the figures into the very guts of the place.

Jessica edged up beside him and waited.

When he was aware of her he did not immediately look round. Instead he smiled to himself and said as though addressing the vast grey-green panel before him:

'How very agreeable. How pleasant to have company.'

Jessica glanced over her shoulder at the two men in white overalls at the central table. They were comparing two large charts. Like Schroeder, they lived in a world of their own.

'Mr Dampier sent this.' She spoke more sharply than she had meant to. She refused to treat this place like a cathedral.

Schroeder took the folded timetable from her and opened it.

'So.'

'Mr Dampier feels that this will be an easier programme to operate,' said Jessica, although Dampier had expressed no such feelings and had certainly not asked her to convey such a message to Schroeder.

'Mr Dampier is asserting the rights of the office desk above those of the laboratory bench?'

'I don't think he — '

'My dear Miss Rogers.' His smile was simian. 'We know Mr Dampier of old.'

And he, she thought, knows you too.

'Shall I tell him it's all in order?' she asked.

'Oh, dear, no. Not at once. I shall have to give the matter some thought. You will realise, Miss Rogers, that I did not send my amended timetable to Mr Dampier purely as a joke.'

'Of course not.'

'It had been carefully evolved. The same care will have to be applied to Mr Dampier's own alternatives.'

Out of the blue it came to her that she must soon leave Intersyn and find a job somewhere else.

It was an alarming thought. Few people left Intersyn of their own accord. Few people even contemplated the idea. Yet all at once she knew that she was tired of the whole silly game. She was tired of watching these men jockeying for position, juggling with prestige, and bristling like little dogs at every threat to their status. It was all so suave and so deadly. There was so much talk of Company spirit and so little about the reality of men and women. The individuals had no more awareness of one another, no more liking for one another, than the dials and convoluted circuits of these control panels had for the materials whose vagaries they recorded. They observed, they recorded, they planned ahead: behind the dials and behind the human faces the facts clicked into place and the plans were evolved; but there was no such thing as a living relationship.

She said: 'Perhaps you'll ring Mr Dampier and let him know what you think.'

'Yes, I think I will do that.' Schroeder dismissed her by turning back to the panel. 'I am busy now, but perhaps in the morning I will ring Mr Dampier.'

She could have said that the morning would be too late, but she was sure that was what he wanted her to say and that he already had a response prepared to slide under her ribs. So she said: 'Good night.'

As she turned away, one of the men with the chart looked across the room. At the same time a quiet bell began to ring, soft yet surprisingly penetrating.

Schroeder swung round. He was at

once horrified but excited.

'Look — what the hell . . . ?'

One of the men slid across the floor towards a dial whose red finger had hammered suddenly over, slamming desperately as though trapped at six o'clock.

Schroeder cried: 'The extrusion plant!'

The three men were on their way to the door. Jessica found herself hurrying after them.

'But it can't have jammed — not with all the other readings consistent . . .'

'Ought to have tripped.'

She could never be sure, afterwards, that she had really heard that despairing, wailing sound which died into the placid evening. She could not swear that she had been able to identify it as what was left of a human scream. But there was something. There was a cry lost on the air. Of that she was sure at the time and not sure later.

One of the control room assistants reached the building first and jerked open the door. He dashed to the far end of the machine, and what he saw there made him grab for the emergency switch.

'No!' yelled Schroeder.

He was too late.

There might be criticism afterwards. Whenever a man dies there is always a voice to say that this should have been done or that not done. But the action was instinctive. Anyone would have done the same.

In any case, it was out of the question that the man who had fallen from the catwalk into the plastic lava should have been still alive.

He was spreadeagled in the stuff. It had surged up and around and over him. When the switch was thrown the abrupt change of temperature had an immediate effect. The glutinous material solidified at once, squeezing slightly as it did so, flattening and distorting the body and then providing it with a transparent casing.

Philip Western was a fly in amber — a fly slightly scorched, slightly squashed, with the discharge from burst blood vessels and dragged flesh staining his face and clothes, preserved for ever.

8

The police were very tactful. One would hardly have known they were there. They examined the iron walk and the extrusion plant, and the Factory Inspector was summoned quickly to do the same. The incident was an unfortunate one but there was no reason to suppose there had been any criminal intent.

Had anyone known that Western was in the plant that evening? Nobody. Was there any reason why he should have been? No official reason.

Was there anyone with a grudge against him?

Every member of the Course was asked this, just as a matter of routine. In every case the answer was no.

The Company presented its featureless, corporate face to the world. There had been a regrettable accident. Publicity would do nobody any good. Western's family would be compensated in spite of the fact that he had had no business to be there in the first place. The Company prided itself on its safety regulations. In two previous cases of death — one in a fire, one in the laminates plant — it had been proved beyond the possibility of doubt that the fault had been that of the operatives concerned. It was almost impossible to have an accident at Belby: you had to be wantonly careless to do so.

It was not the Company's fault. And of course it was nothing so melodramatic as murder. Just the inexplicable carelessness of a Course member who ought to have known better than to lean too far over a railing. A promising man, too. A great disappointment to the Company.

Partridge himself addressed the Course members.

He was a stocky man with blue-veined cheeks and a mass of very dry brown hair. He wore heavy horn-rimmed glasses and kept them as a rule pushed up on to his forehead. This gave him an air of being harassed yet of being always able to cope. His lower lip was brutal, his jaw too broad.

He said: 'You all know what's happened. It has been a great blow to all of us. My first address to this Executive Course was meant to be given under more cheerful circumstances.'

His whole tone accused the dead man of disloyalty.

'We'll never know what happened to Western. Never know why he fell. Can't ask you to forget it, of course, but I do ask you not to waste too much time thinking about it. And don't gossip about it. I know it'll be a strain when you hear people talking about it. You'll want to say 'Oh, that happened on the Course that I was on.' Don't. You're senior men. You've got something better to do than gossip.'

His head was too large for his body. It turned ponderously as he studied them one by one. He took his time. He was a Director. They could sit and wait while he did things the way he wanted to do them.

'Now,' he said, 'let's put this unpleasant business out of our minds. You know the reason why you're here. It hasn't changed. The Course must go on just as before. I expect you to work just as hard as though nothing had happened.'

It was an order. It was a cancelling out of things that tried to interfere with Company policy. Western's death had happened. All right, it had happened; and from now on you declared that it hadn't happened and you went on just as before.

Partridge turned the page. What had been written on the previous page now ceased to exist. He talked without any change of intonation or manner about the responsibilities of management. He talked about staff grading and staff control. He wasted no time on jokes or appeals to their vanity. He made it clear that you became a Director because you knew your job and knew how to use the people under your control. Only he didn't refer to them as people. He spoke of the labour force and of middle management and of top management, of co-ordination of executive skills, and of management ratios and interfirm comparisons. Partridge was a technical man and made no bones about it; but he did not indulge in sly digs at his non-technical fellow Directors as Dampier or Schroeder might have done on their own level. He didn't need to. When he had finished, it was clear that in order to become a Director you had to be a certain kind of General Manager or Department Controller. He told you what the pattern was. It was simple . . . if you could squeeze and twist and bully yourself into that pattern.

It was all cold and lucid and very important. You had to be on your toes if you wanted to get there. You had to be alive.

They were alive: all of them in this room, they were alive. Philip Western was dead. Western was out of it.

The verdict would be accidental death. There could be no other verdict. In a Company of this repute, even an industrial accident of that kind was bad enough. It had to be admitted, lamented, and relegated to the past.

But the local newspaper, an amalgam of some fifteen local papers that had flourished in the early twentieth century and then gradually blended into the one gawkily assembled sixteen-page outpouring of small ads and news items about bazaars, council elections, rights of way and sewage, did recall that there had been a similar accident in the plant some years ago. The Company was distressed by the paragraph, and there would be some enquiries made to the Belby Press Officer as to how this had slipped through. They took the editor out often enough, didn't they? All the local reporters usually referred their material back for friendly checking just to make sure the facts were right, and the implications not damaging, didn't they? There would be a longer inquest on this than on Philip Western.

But the paragraph had appeared. It mentioned one of those incidents that had for years been tucked away in a drawer — forgotten, as it was hoped Western would soon be forgotten.

In the days before that particular building had been converted to the manufacture of the new resin, when the autoclaves and centrifuges had been exposed and noisy and their operation had been controlled by men on the spot instead of by remote, infallible switches and circuits, another highly respected and valued Intersyn employee had fallen to his death from the earlier, more rickety iron walk.

His name was Richard Marsh.

* * *

'Did you know about this?' Andrew demanded.

He flourished the newspaper at her. They were in the saloon bar of a pub on the outskirts of Belby. He had come to her and unexpectedly asked her out for a drink — to get out of the place, to get the smell of it out of their nostrils, he said. He sounded angry. She was used to this. It was the way he sounded when he was doing something he wanted to do but felt that he ought not to want to do it. She wondered why he had broken his rule of abstinence. He was actually taking her out for the evening — to a drab little pub, where the beer was flat and the locals muttered self-sufficiently.

Jessica said: 'I knew that David's father died in an accident. A lot of people know that. The Company has looked after him pretty well as a result of it.'

'All right, it's been pretty well established. But did you know *how* he died? Did you know the accident took place in that plant, just where Western's just copped it?'

'No,' said Jessica, 'I didn't.'

'Some things are hidden even from you?'

'Some things aren't all that relevant.'

'I thought personnel records were complete down to the last detail.'

'The way a man's father died has little bearing on the way the man works.'

'You think not? I'd have thought these circumstances were rather special.'

'What has it got to do with you?'

'Don't put on your Company voice,' said Andrew. 'I know the official line but I don't want to hear it being trotted out by you. We've had it from Partridge and from Dampier. But now from you, Jess, please. You know as well as I do that it's a thumping great coincidence, two men dying on the same spot.'

'A danger spot,' she said. 'Obviously there's something about the lighting, or the rail isn't high enough. Or something.'

'Or something!' he echoed. 'Oh, that's what the Factory Inspector will decide — that a higher rail and less dazzling lighting will somehow do the trick. But the catwalk isn't the same one that was there in Marsh's father's day, and the lights can't be the same. The whole shed was different. Yet Western tips over just the way the other man did. How — and why?'

'It was an accident. We'll never know.'

'That's what they say. They're great at that — 'don't know' and 'no comment'.'

'Andrew,' she said, 'did you invite me out just to harangue me about Western's death?'

'Western's death plus old man Marsh's death.'

'It's old man Marsh who interests you?' she said recklessly. 'The old one — not the young one?'

He slammed his hand down on the table, and beer splashed up out of his glass and spattered across the red plastic top. Keeping his voice down he said:

'Look, Jess, I don't like that sort of talk.

It's cheap. It's not like you. Anyone would think you'd got something to be proud of in . . . well, anyway . . . '

'Or is it just so that you won't look too conspicuous? A double game — the calculation of the really promising Course member. If you avoid me too much it will show, won't it? All the other men on the Course talk to me and ask me out, so you think you'd better do it. Is that what you've decided?'

It was true that at this stage the men usually relaxed slightly. Feeling school-boyish because they were so far from their normal haunts they would try their luck with Jessica. She allowed some of them to take her out. Some escorts talked shop as though suspecting her of being still on duty and liable to report back on their behaviour and conversation. Others tried to show their scorn for such tactics but nevertheless proved that they felt precisely the same by employing another technique: they did not mention the Company at all. It was a great strain when they were like that.

Jessica was rarely asked to go to bed

with any of them. They were too wary.

Andrew leaned forward, his sleeve resting against the edge of a puddle of beer. Jessica watched the cloth darkening but could not bring herself to draw his attention to it.

He said: 'Jess, this Course is just something that's got to be lived through. It's got to be got out of the way. And when it is — couldn't we manage a holiday together?'

She looked at his hand around the beer glass. She hardly dared to meet his eyes. In a second he had conjured up a picture that was too beautiful and too painful. Trust Andrew! He had only to say something like that, and she was right back in the world he had created for her. She remembered the long weekend they had managed together last year — and the incredible week the year before that, the week that she had known even then could never be repeated. Now, when she had felt herself drifting carefully and silently away from him, hoping he would not notice until the distance between them was too great for him even to call after her, he had reached out and pulled her back.

'Once it's over,' he said, 'we'll know where we are. We can make plans.'

Once it was over. He was making it plain that the Course still had top priority in his thoughts. He was going to go through with it.

'Plans?' she said despondently. 'What plans?'

She knew that she was a fool to be so expectant. However weary she might allow herself to feel, she was waiting for him to prove to her that everything could somehow be made right. There were a dozen ways in which he might say it if he wanted to say it.

Andrew drank deeply and sighed. 'You know what this infernal rat race is like.'

He tried to sound as though he hated the whole thing but it was the pose that all of them adopted. He still intended to emerge at the head of the pack. And when he had succeeded, what promises would he make? What thoughts would he have of her? Second thoughts, no doubt.

'A drink?' he said, finishing his glass.

'No, thanks.'

'Sure?'

'I think we ought to be getting back.'

'You've got a date?'

'No,' said Jessica, 'I haven't got a date.'

They walked back to the hostel in silence. The towers and chimneys of the plant stood up against the sky like a cluster of harsh spires and towers above a severely functional city. Few people moved in the streets. In the daytime the men worked in the plant, the women did their shopping; in the evening they were at home watching television.

Andrew and Jessica walked below the long, curving wall that shielded the secrets of Intersyn from the outside world. It was blank for a couple of hundred yards save for a number of small metal doors and one unexpectedly ornamental iron gate which allowed a view into the twinkling heart of the place — sparkling with lights although nobody was in sight.

Andrew moved abruptly away from Jessica towards the wall and said: 'Hold it. Isn't that . . . ?'

He stood against the wall, dissociating himself from her. She watched the heavy, dark shape of Bill Crowther cross the road some way ahead of them. He glanced quickly in their direction but she could not be sure that he had seen them. Then he seemed to vanish into the wall.

'It *was* Crowther?' said Andrew.

'Yes. It was Crowther.'

They walked slowly on, and found another door in the wall. Andrew pushed it gently, but it would not open.

'He must have let himself out that way, and then let himself in and locked it again,' he said. 'But why? What's he up to?'

Jessica stood back and looked up at the surface of the wall. She tried to visualise the interior of the factory, working out its layout step by step. The main gate was in the imposing frontage, on the far side from here. The laboratories . . . admin offices . . . she paced her way mentally over the site. Then she said:

'This entrance could be a useful short cut to the hostel.'

'But why should Crowther want his

own special exit and entrance? And how does he come to be using it?'

'He used to work here. Probably knows every side door in the place. And' — Jessica tried to laugh it off, wondering why she was so uneasy about Crowther's oddly furtive dash across the road — 'I expect he gets a kick out of showing off, even if only to himself.'

Andrew came to the edge of the pavement beside her and looked up at the wall.

'Yes. He spent a long time here — belongs up here, really, doesn't he? Maybe he's got an old girl-friend in the town.'

'An old flame,' Jessica agreed. It robbed the incident of importance if you made a conventional joke out of it.

'A bit far away for normal use. Up here, the embers can't get breathed on all that often.'

'Not only up here,' said Jessica involuntarily.

Beside her, Andrew stiffened and went on staring up at the barrier of brick.

'She's not the only one,' said Jessica.

'Further south, it's just the same.'

Andrew said, 'What else is there over this wall — on the other side, right opposite?'

'I can't be absolutely sure.'

He heard the betraying note in her voice. 'You can,' he accused her.

'The extrusion plant, I think.'

'You're sure?'

'No, not really.'

'You're sure,' he said. 'Then what the hell . . . '

'There are plenty of doors. Plenty of ways in and out of the plant.'

'All locked from the inside,' said Andrew, 'unless you know how to operate them. Crowther . . . how often do you suppose he comes this way? And does he go right through the extrusion plant shed, or round it, and does he meet anyone on the way — and if so, what happens to them?'

Jessica walked on. He caught up with her. They went in through the main gate and under an archway of gleaming pipes and reached the hostel. They said good night with such bleak formality that any casual witness might have supposed that Andrew had made a pass at her and been slapped down.

Jessica went to her room and lay down on the bed. She longed for sleep but for a few minutes could not summon up the energy to undress.

Her room was painted in an austere pink. The lamp shade was a deeper, restful red. She turned away from the light and looked at the picture on the wall. It was an enlargement of a black and white photograph of Intersyn's main German subsidiary, the gleaming new plant set against a background of hills and what looked like steeply sloping vineyards.

There was a tap at her door.

Jessica swung her legs off the bed.

'Hello?'

It could only be Dampier, fussing over some little detail which must be changed. The recent tragedy would have had no great effect on the feud between himself and Schroeder.

It was not until her hand was on the door knob that she wondered, startlingly yet dispassionately, if Dampier had pushed Western.

She opened the door, hoping her face would not give her away.

David stood outside. 'Can I come in?'

'David — you oughtn't to be here.'

'I want to talk to you.'

'We could have a drink downstairs, or sit in the lounge.'

'No,' he said. 'I want to talk to you alone. There's nobody else I can talk to.'

She stood back and he came in. She expected him to kiss her but he walked straight past. When she closed the door he sat on the bed and stared at her. She waved at a chair. He paid no attention. Her room had a desk, a table, several chairs and a couch; but he sat on the bed and looked at her until she came and sat beside him. She waited for him to put his arm round her.

He said, 'What do you make of it?'

'Of what?'

'Western's death,' he said keenly, probingly.

Jessica sighed. Partridge and Dampier might lecture as much as they liked, there would be only one topic of conversation now until the Course was ended — and perhaps beyond it.

'It was an accident. I thought that had been established.'

'Established?' he said. 'By whom?'

'Do we have to talk about it?' said Jessica. A few minutes ago she had been sprawling on the bed, longing for peace. Now she wanted even more to sleep. If he wanted to make love to her before she went to sleep, she wouldn't resist — she didn't really want him tonight, but at the same time she was hurt that for him too there was only one thing to talk about, only one topic he wanted to discuss with her. Let him come into bed with her and then let there be sleep. She said: 'Is that all you can talk about?'

'It's not surprising. My father died in the same place. It didn't strike you as odd?'

'Well — '

'It strikes everyone else as odd,' said David. 'I can see by the way they look at me.'

'I think they're probably embarrassed.

Not wanting to mention it, but finding it awkward to skate round. You must know how it feels.'

'I ought to,' he said: 'it's a subject I've had to spend half my life skating round.'

'I hadn't realised it meant so much to you.' She was stricken by that faraway expression of his as he sat there and waited, it seemed, for her verdict. Her verdict on what? He was a small boy again, waiting. It was difficult to tell whether he waited for punishment or solace. She thought of his mother, and his mother's only compelling subject of conversation. She said: 'I suppose that accident altered so many things for you. It must have had a terrible effect on your life . . . your way of life. One doesn't think.'

'Accident?' he said. 'My father was murdered.'

*   *   *

This was the story he had come to tell her. 'There's nobody else I can talk to.' So he talked to Jessica. He told her a story with a frightening inner logic and a surface of frightening fantasy. It had to be fantasy.

At first he had been grateful to Intersyn for their generosity following his father's death. It had been made subtly apparent to him that he had cause for gratitude. He owed his education to Intersyn and in due course he was offered an excellent position in the firm. Things were made easy for him. His mother was the only person who didn't tell him repeatedly how lucky he was.

His mother's cryptic remarks about its being a lot less than he deserved were restrained at first. She was perhaps stunned by the loss of her husband. While the teachers and friends and the Intersyn Welfare Officer told David how fortunate he was, his mother told him what a wonderful man his father had been; and this tied in with David's memories well enough. Then his mother began to speak more freely — only to him, of course. She saved the long explanations until he was old enough to grasp them. At the end of his first year with Intersyn she told him that the new development which was making a fortune for the Company had been his father's. Richard Marsh had originated the early experiments, carried them through . . . and then been robbed of victory. Mrs Marsh remembered his exultation, remembered him scribbling in that notebook of his, and remembered his declaration that he had solved it — had made the final definitive step. He was a Company employee, he wouldn't get any more money for it — not in cash, not paid over just like that — but the prestige of having achieved what they had been struggling to synthesise for so long, and the eventual promotion that this must mean, were a glowing promise for him.

Then he died. His notebook disappeared. Partridge, the Departmental Head who had been working with him and with Dr Schroeder, got the main credit. In due course he also got a Directorship. Partridge was that kind of man. And Partridge must have killed Richard Marsh.

'My father didn't fall off that catwalk by accident,' David said to Jessica. 'He knew everything about that plant — the inside and outside of every vessel, every little thing that could happen. He must have been killed.'

Jessica's mouth was dry. All she could say was, 'It couldn't happen.'

'It did happen.'

'You've no proof.'

'No,' said David, 'but I'm going to get it. That's why I'm here. That's why I'm on this Course.'

For a wild moment, trapped in the lurid nightmare of his aberration, she thought he meant that he had been given a place on this Course by the management solely on the grounds that he wished to unearth evidence of their own treachery.

'No,' she said. 'They must have put you on it because they thought you were good. You're on it because —

'Because I dropped some unpleasant hints,' he said.

'Hints?'

'I told them that they weren't treating me fairly,' said David. And then, very earnestly, very anxious that he should see

204

this was still straightforward and above reproach, he added: 'And it was true. I wouldn't have tackled it that way if I hadn't felt absolutely right about it. I said I wasn't getting a fair deal — I was just a charity case. I wanted to get on the Executive Course — mainly to get close to these people, of course, but also because I deserved it as much as anyone did. And they had to let me come on it.'

Jessica, steeped in the ethics of personnel procedure in Intersyn, said: 'They don't usually let candidates tell them about their own suitability.'

'Not usually,' David agreed. 'But in this case they felt it would be a good thing to send me on the Course . . . so that charity was not only done but could be seen to be done.'

'But why did you think the Course was so important? So important to your theory about your father, I mean.'

David had felt that he would have to get close before he could prove anything. He wanted to mix with the people in power, to listen to Schroeder and try to catch him out, to see Partridge and see if

205

he could be made to falter; to come to Belby and check.

'Check?' said Jessica. 'On what?'

He knew when the patent for the new resin had been taken out. He knew that its development was blurred over as a communal enterprise in the official booklets issued to staff. He knew, because his mother had told him over and over again, that his father's black notebook had disappeared — a notebook so well known to his colleagues and everyone else that it was a standing joke, as Schroeder himself had made clear on this very Course. David wanted to find out. He wanted to catch somebody out. He wanted to see somebody frightened, and then to go after him.

David's voice rose as he talked. There was a stage at which Jessica tried to stop him, afraid of people hearing and of sly stories going around; but then the whole impossible story that David was telling became more real and overpowering than all other conceivable stories added together, and she listened to him and forgot about anyone outside.

'Somebody,' he said, 'must have been scared stiff when he learnt I was on this Course. That's what I've been banking on. Partridge, I think. Or someone very close to him. Partridge or Schroeder? They never expected me to get this far. Charity was all right — a nice little sinecure somewhere, provided by the Company so that a few consciences could be eased — but I wasn't expected to work so hard that I could force my way on to the Executive Course. It must have been a shock. A shock . . . for somebody.'

And that somebody, thought Jessica, appointed a spy to keep watch on David Marsh and see that he didn't get too close. She was conscious of a queasy feeling. If anything was sure in these shifting sands of speculation, it was that Philip Western had been Partridge's man, Partridge's appointed spy.

Philip Western was dead. He had died at the same spot as that where David's father died.

Because he knew too much?

David, still sitting on the bed, pressing his feet very lightly against the floor every now and then so that he swayed backwards and downwards into the softness of the bed, knew what was in her mind. She was suddenly aware of this. He said:

'Which brings us to Mr Western, doesn't it?'

'David . . . you didn't, did you?'

'I didn't what?' He looked rather amused, and much more adult than the little boy who had been sitting there a few minutes ago.

She forced herself to say it. 'You didn't push Philip Western over the rail in order to provide a . . . well, a sort of vengeful parallel to what happened . . . what you think happened to your father?'

'No,' he said. 'No, I didn't do that.'

The absurdity of her question hit her as she swayed against his shoulder. If Western had known anything, David would have been keen to keep him alive.

And when she had thought that, she realised that she was half assuming that David's story was true. If Western had *known* anything . . . Known what? What was there to know? A resentful accusation dreamed up by a sad widow, fed into her son's mind — and David had been convincing enough to make her wonder what Western knew and what Partridge had done.

She said: 'You can't believe it, surely? You can't think there's anything in it — stealing an idea, committing murder, setting a highly-placed spy on you?'

'Yes. I do believe it. I'm sure of it.'

'But . . .'

She thought of the men she had known in the Company. She thought of the Partridges and the Dampiers, the men from overseas and the drab little schemers in London office. With a jolt she thought of Andrew.

She knew that David could be right. They were capable of deceit. They were capable of the slow sapping of a man's power and of his self-respect. There was no reason why they should not be capable of murder. If murder became necessary they would find excuses to justify it to themselves, just as they justified other things by the circulation of interminable memoranda written in agonisingly constipated prose.

'But,' she said, 'what can you hope to do?'

'To expose the truth. Someone will give himself away sooner or later.'

'Do you think so?'

'Yes. It all started here in Belby. Someone here will drop a remark, or get frightened and blurt out a wrong date or a wrong fact or . . . or something. And then I'll know.'

'But even then, what do you do about it?'

'If I can show everyone the truth, they'll believe it,' said David simply.

'The truth,' Jessica echoed. 'But there's more to it than that. It takes a lot of proving. Just exposing it — just saying 'Look, there it is' . . . that's not enough.'

'But it must be.'

She put her hand on his, hoping he would turn the palm towards her. He sat quite still.

' 'The truth is great and shall prevail'?' said Jessica softly.

'Yes.' He was delighted that there should be such an apposite quotation.

'You know the next line?'

'No.'

' 'When none cares whether it prevail or not.' '

'But *I* care,' he said with quiet intensity. And now he turned his hand and gripped hers tightly. 'Jessica, I want you to understand. I want you to know. You've got to believe me — you've got to be with me on this.'

It meant such a lot to him. His conviction of rightness was communicated to her like an electrical charge through his fingertips. She felt like saying 'Yes, yes' and nodding and promising and at the same time she was sorry for him: it was so naive, so schoolboyishly pure and idealistic, his belief that to state the self-evident truth was enough for it to be accepted. The ways of the world were more devious than that. But she sensed that if she told him this he would say simply that they ought not to be; that the world itself must be altered.

He was sure. Yet he needed her reassurance.

She said: 'But the idea that Partridge

would put an important man like Western on the Course simply to spy on you — '

'It would have to be someone big, wouldn't it? He couldn't trust anyone lower down the scale — and in any case it would have been difficult to get anyone of lesser importance on to the Course. I'm willing to bet Western came on at the last minute, after it was known that the London office had put me on it. He did, didn't he?'

'Well . . . '

'You know something about it,' he said. 'You know, don't you, Jess?'

What she knew, or thought she had known, was that Western had been watching Dampier. She had told Dampier this.

'What is it?' said David urgently.

Western had been watching David Marsh, but they had thought he was watching Dampier. Western had exchanged rooms with Bill Crowther in the London hotel not to be next to Dampier, but to be next to David. It was David's room he had investigated — deliberately, and not by mistake as she had thought at the time.

It could be her fault that Western was dead. Dampier, believing himself to be under surveillance, could have pushed Western over that rail.

Fantastic. But no more fantastic than David's suspicions. No more fantastic than the whole grotesque game of the Executive Course itself. When nerves were stretched as though on a gruelling battle course, casualties were all too likely. When you were trained to play a dangerous game for high stakes you might well decide to take the ultimate gamble.

'What is it?' said David again.

'I'm trying to sort it all out in my mind,' she said weakly.

He accepted this. His fingers slackened their grip. He was perhaps a little disappointed, as though he had been hoping that with a few phrases, a few neat revelations, she would have been able to solve all his doubts. He said: 'You'll keep a lookout for me, won't you? You're in the middle of it all. Someone's bound to say something. Dampier. Or someone. And if anyone makes a slip, tell me. Tell me everything — and if there is a slip anywhere, I'll recognise it.' He gave her a diffident smile. 'After all, I've been studying the subject for years!'

Jessica realised suddenly how late it was. David ought not to be here in her room at this hour. Unless, she thought incongruously, he intended to stay the night. She looked markedly at her watch and said: 'You really must be going. Or . . . ' And she left the rest to him.

David got up and looked solemnly down at her. With great deliberation he said:

'I think I love you, Jessica.'

She wanted to laugh. Then she wanted to cry. Then she just felt unutterably weary and wished he would go so that she could lie down and sleep.

'When this business is over,' he was saying, 'we'll have time to talk about it, won't we? You want to talk about it, don't you? You know what I'm trying to say.'

Time to talk, she thought. So much talk. And David so scrupulous. He only *thought* he loved her. He was too meticulous to commit himself further than that. When this business was over . . . Would it ever be over? The months and years of Andrew, with Andrew promising and half promising things in the future. But the future never came. That was one thing she had learnt: the future would always be the future, darting away ahead of you, always just that little bit more than an arm's length away so that you could never grasp it.

So David thought he loved her and vaguely he thought they might talk about it when all this was over. And when all this was over there would be something else.

Or would David be different? David at least had no wife to impede him — or to serve as an excuse for comfortable evasiveness.

'It's late,' she said. 'You'd better go.'

He kissed her and went.

A passionless kiss. You can do better than that, she silently accused him after he had gone. Come back and try again. Then she forced herself to go quickly to bed before she should start to want him too much.

And lying there wide awake, she grimly

admitted that she was no better than the rest of them. It was no good accusing Andrew or David. The place and the people obsessed her, too. She wanted to know how the Course would turn out, what Partridge had done or not done in the past, what had happened to David Marsh's father, and what had happened to Philip Western.

Dampier had been very anxious to get rid of her that evening. Even at the time she had thought it was unusual that he should send her to see Schroeder instead of going himself. He had wanted her out of the way. What was it he had said? Something about seeing someone . . . or having something to do . . .

She would not make a good witness in a court of law. The exact words escaped her. But she was left with a vivid recollection of Dampier's manner and of his fidgety determination to send her off on that errand, to get rid of her for a short time.

During that short time Philip Western had died.

9

Dampier said: 'During the last few days you have seen the technical background to our worldwide operations. We have tried to build up for you a clear picture of the whole Intersyn organisation. I hope you see how all the pieces fit together. The whole,' he said lamely, 'is the sum of the parts.'

Andrew thought that Dampier was looking very pale. He spoke without his usual bland conviction. There were no jokes about the technical boys and no sly implications that he, Dampier, really held all the threads in his own hands.

'At this stage,' he went on, 'we usually have a discussion on Forward Planning. As you will have realised during your visits to the various processes, it is no good simply turning out material in vast quantities. The fact that we can produce several million miles of synthetic fibre more cheaply than anyone else in

Western Europe is of little significance if there is no demand for such fibre. You will have noted that a new plant is standing idle in one corner of the factory while an older and less efficient building is working to capacity. But the newer process will play its part again within a few months. There was a temporary recession for which our planners had not allowed. Now we have been able to estimate future needs and balance our programme accordingly.

'Forward Planning is essential in all industry today. It is not enough to guess what the public will be needing two years from now: if you guess, and go in for a new scheme of building plant and offices, you are liable to find that you have concentrated on a product which is on its way to being obsolete. New techniques are being developed all the time. New demands are being made by industrially advanced countries and by the emergent nations. Intersyn has to be able to calculate far ahead what the demands will be and to adjust its supply. Just as it would be silly for an oil refinery to concentrate on building expensive distillation and cracking plant with the emphasis on producing more and more gasoline, only to find that the demand is for increased quantities of heavy fuel oil, so it could be disastrous for Intersyn to get over-enthusiastic about one particular product, however profitable it may seem at the moment, if there is likely to be a demand for something different a year from now. We have to plan ahead. We have to decide today, as accurately as possible, what plant and raw materials and staff we shall need six months, a year, two years from now.'

Dampier stopped. In previous lectures he had often looked round the class at such a juncture, waiting for a question or smiling like an actor who hears applause, even if only in his own head. Now he seemed to falter. He had stopped because he had lost his way.

Unexpectedly, he said: 'Er, yes.' It was an incantation, an appeal to the Muses to inspire him once more.

Hornbrook helped him out. Suavely he asked: 'You mentioned staff requirements.

I think that would be of particular interest to all of us.' He looked round and there was a general murmur of agreement. 'Forecasting of staff distribution is a key point in management — it would be a great help to us . . . ' Hornbrook let the sentence trail gently away so that Dampier could take it up.

Gratefully Dampier responded to the cue. 'Absolutely. For most of you, staff questions will loom much larger than the purely technical ones of material and flow adjustment. Though they are, of course, linked. When our Forward Planning Analysts predict output requirements for the coming years, they also feed staff data into the computers. It must seem strange to some employees that Intersyn often declares certain people redundant while at the same time advertising widely for new staff. But we have to be realistic about such matters. It may seem harsh to some . . . '

Andrew found himself feeling sorry for Dampier. It was quite pathetic. Although he was talking fluently enough now, Dampier lacked the strength that he had shown at the beginning of the Course. He was saying familiar words and conveying ideas that he must have put across a hundred times before; but there was an undertone of doubt, almost of reproach. He was in danger of becoming an agnostic. Andrew wondered what had happened to him: who had hit him, and where?

'It had always been part of the Course at Belby,' Dampier plodded on, 'to show how these questions of demand and supply are assessed. In the last year, however, more and more of the calculations have been taken over by London. The installation of new computers last year has made a great difference to the whole sequence of operations, and on the whole we think you will get a clearer idea of the work if we shift that discussion period to London. We'll spend our last day here showing what actually happens when the statistics come in from Head Office — how process programming is adjusted in a few specific instances — and then you can fit this all in with what we see when we get back to London.

'And speaking of getting back to London, I have a little piece of news for you.' Dampier made a gallant effort to revive his roguish manner. 'In view of the curtailing of the programme here — and, to be frank, in view of the recent unpleasant occurrence which has distressed us all — we have decided to allow you all a little treat.' He smirked graciously. When it came to passing on a decision from the authorities, Dampier was skilled in implying that some of the credit for the decision rested with him. 'Instead of travelling down to London on Sunday and reporting straight to the hotel, you can leave late Friday afternoon and have a weekend at home. The Course will be resumed first thing on Monday morning, so it would be advisable for you to report to the hotel late on Sunday unless you can be sure of reaching the lecture room straight from home on Monday morning.'

There was a gratifying surge of comment. Dampier nodded, his self-possession somewhat restored. Computers might work out as many impersonal schemes as they liked, planning for the intake of brash young science graduates and for the ditching of the old pioneers who had built Intersyn up to what it was today; but it was the Dampiers of the world who added the human touch, handling men firmly but knowing just how to donate half holidays and pats on the head.

During the morning tea break there was a scramble for the two telephones provided for private use in the rest room.

Dampier, drinking from a very large cup which he affected and of which there was an equivalent in London office, went on nodding benignly.

'I think,' he said to Ames, 'we all need a day or two to readjust.'

Ames was delighted to be singled out for the honour of this communication. He agreed. Fervently he agreed. It was very thoughtful . . . very sensible . . . excellent policy. Yes indeed. Time to readjust.

Men telephoned their wives and said they would be home on Friday evening or in the small hours of Saturday. A couple made jokes about turfing the lodger out of bed — but not too loudly, in case this was not in the accepted tradition of Company jokes. Blackwell, whose wife had gone away with the children for a fortnight, made plans to stay with a cousin and see a show.

Hornbrook said to Andrew: 'It's free now.'

'Hm?' Andrew had been staring out of the window at the impeccable brightness of the laboratory window frames across the courtyard.

'The telephone,' said Hornbrook. 'There's one free now if you want to ring home.'

'Oh. Yes, thanks.' Andrew moved towards it and then said, though there was no reason why he should make excuses to Hornbrook: 'I think I'll leave it till later. No great rush.'

The next lecture was one of those dry, uninspiring ones to which they all listened with impassive faces. One man's eyelids drooped and his head sagged gently forward from time to time. A sympathetic colleague nudged him each time just as his head was about to plump down on to the desk. Andrew stifled a succession of yawns. Dampier was sitting in on the lecture at the back of the room. If he knew his job, he would report that this lecturer was not up to the task and should be sent back into his department to get on with useful work in future. Some people could put across their subject with clarity and enthusiasm; some, good in their own field, were unable to explain even the simplest points. This chap was hopeless.

At the end of the lecture Jessica came in with some notes for Dampier. They stood a few feet away from Andrew. He looked at her, willing her to return his gaze. Once she glanced at him and half smiled, but that was all. He knew what he intended to do this coming weekend. But he must get to her before that young Marsh did.

The sight of her angered him. She could be so elusive when she wished to be. And then, when you caught her and enjoyed her, she would become clinging and just as exasperating in a completely different way. He didn't know why he wanted her. All he felt was that Marsh wasn't going to have her. He was going to prove to her this weekend that she wasn't meant for Marsh.

He met her on the way to the Senior Mess in the lunch hour.

'You heard about us going home for the weekend.'

'Of course.'

'Yes, of course, you would.' He kept his smile pleasant and comradely so that if anyone passed there would be nothing to provoke comment. 'I was thinking what a nice little gift it was.'

'Were you?' Jessica's hazel eyes seemed not to blink. They appraised him dispassionately as though she were making herself see him for the first time.

Andrew was suddenly afraid that she would say no. Already it might be too late. It became imperative that things should work out as he wanted them to. He had made a decision — the sort of decision she always wanted him to make, the sort she had hinted at before the Course began — and now she must fall in with it.

He said: 'Shall I come to the flat this weekend, Jess?'

'Oh.' It was no kind of answer — just a sigh.

'It seems too good an opportunity to miss, doesn't it?'

'I hadn't thought of it like that.'

'It was the first thing I thought of when Dampier told us.'

'Was it?' she said wonderingly.

'Damn it, Jess' — he kept his voice down but now he saw her blink as she recognised the note of violence — 'you were the one who said we ought to be able to organise something on the Course. And now here's a splendid opportunity.'

'I suppose so.'

'Muriel won't know,' he said. 'She's not expecting me back this weekend anyway. I don't have to ring her — don't have to do a thing. Except come to you. Isn't that what you want?'

'I don't know,' said Jessica. 'But let's try it and see.'

'Not what I'd call a warm invitation.'

'The invitation came from you,' said Jessica. 'As to the warmth . . . let's see if it's still there when we reach London, shall we?'

Jessica hated his glib assumption that she would fall in so readily with his plans. Because it suited Andrew to climb into her bed this weekend, she was expected to agree automatically. Muriel wouldn't know, so that made everything all right — almost respectable, one could have gathered from Andrew's manner. The fact that he did not have to telephone her and invent excuses meant a lot to him. Naturally he would consider it normal and logical to take advantage of such a situation when it was presented to him.

She wondered what she would say if David now asked her to go down to his home, even if only for an afternoon.

The question did not arise. When they next met he said that he had been out into the town for a few drinks, meeting some of his father's old friends in a pub and sounding them out. Jessica was alarmed. It would do him no good if it came to the ears of Partridge and others that he was asking awkward questions about certain Intersyn patents and trying to dig up secrets from the past.

David reassured her. It was all right: he

knew what he was doing. He was being cautious. It was a jigsaw puzzle and he needed a lot of pieces yet. But when he had assembled as many pieces as he could find, the shape of the missing ones might be more easily established.

And as for her, what had she discovered? Hadn't she got a lead for him yet? Surely, talking to Dampier, leading him on to reminisce . . .

Jessica was unhappy at the idea of becoming a snooper and at the same time felt guilty that she should have done so little to help David. Then she revolted against the absurdity of his whole theory. It wasn't just that she couldn't help him: she had no business even to try, no business to encourage him in his lurid interpretations of Intersyn history.

But when they were marking up the Course members' record cards that evening, she held one out thoughtfully and said to Dampier:

'I see there's no mention of the accident on here.'

'Accident?' Dampier looked up, his pencil poised.

'David Marsh's father. His accident. There's no record of it in David Marsh's file.'

'No.'

'Unusual, isn't it? We usually have everything here.'

'I imagine it was considered irrelevant. Nothing to do with the boy's own ability, after all.' Dampier seemed anxious to finish the conversation. He looked down again and slowly, meaningly lowered the pencil.

Jessica said: 'I'd have thought something like that in one's family background was highly relevant.'

Dampier was curt. 'There must have been good reasons for the decision.'

'There might come a time when someone trying to assess his suitability for certain jobs would turn him down for the wrong reasons. He might seem a bit brash, or a bit awkward — particularly if he was asked something about his views on personnel relations, pensions, family traditions in a firm, and so on. A note on the file would surely help any executive to understand his reactions at such a time.'

Dampier pushed himself abruptly back in his chair. 'You seem very interested in young Marsh.'

'I was curious, that's all. You know how used one gets to these records — and how anything out of the ordinary strikes one immediately.'

As soon as she had spoken she realised that this was perhaps not the most fortunate way of putting things. It would be surprising if Dampier's mind was not thrown back on to Philip Western and the suspicions they had had of him. She wondered if she dare hint, ever so obliquely, at David Marsh's certainty that the watcher had been set on *him*. Dampier's reaction would be terribly important. If he had killed Western, thinking himself pursued, and now learnt that Western had been shadowing someone else . . .

But if she told Dampier this, she would implicitly be accepting the truth of David's theories. Half of her mind accepted it already; the other half sought for modifications, for errors of reasoning.

Dampier said: 'We've always worked

pretty well together, haven't we, Miss Rogers?' She was surprised by his suddenly friendly, appealing tone. And now he switched diffidently to her Christian name, as he had done only once or twice before. 'Miss Rogers . . . Jessica . . . perhaps I may be allowed to show some — ah — paternal interest in you. Or shall we say avuncular, anyway?' Dampier smiled rather coyly and began to tap his pencil against his left thumb-nail. 'It is not for me to criticise any relationship you may have with young Marsh. Indeed, I am chary of even commenting on it, let alone criticising. If at some time . . . ah . . . no, let us not speculate.'

He seemed to be nerving himself to say something, but had lost either the thread of his thoughts or his courage. It had happened several times today.

Jessica said: 'Is there something wrong?'

'Wrong? No, nothing wrong. Not now. It's all over — over many years ago.'

Jessica tensed. She could hardly hope that Dampier would unload terrible secrets upon her. It was too much to expect. He wasn't going to clear up the whole mystery, point the finger of accusation at Partridge, and then dictate a tearful confession.

'Mr Marsh's death,' she prompted him. She waited a moment, then said: 'The accident.'

'It was no accident.'

She heard an echo of David's words ringing in her head. No accident, Dampier had just said. And she waited for him to say, as David had said, that David Marsh's father had been murdered.

Dampier said: 'He committed suicide.'

'But . . . that's impossible.'

'Why is it impossible?'

She struggled for common sense in the middle of this new fantasy. 'Why should he have committed suicide?'

'People do.'

'Not when they're working hard at something and within sight of success. No scientist, no writer, no painter, getting that close and knowing he was close, would give up.'

'So that's the story you've been told, is it?' said Dampier gently. 'He died just before he could reach his goal — and someone else claimed the fruits of victory.'

Jessica did not correct him. She did not say that the fruits of victory had been snatched by a murderer. Instead, she said again:

'Why should he have committed suicide?'

'Because he had failed,' said Dampier; 'or thought he had failed.'

'What? But he hadn't. We know — '

'We know,' said Dampier, 'that the team was on the right lines and that the final breakthrough came only a few days later. It's tragic, but things do happen like that. Richard Marsh had been overworking, he was in a highly nervous state — I knew him tolerably well, and you can take it from me that he was very highly strung . . . a very unstable person. He was brilliant in his own field, but there was always the danger of his cracking up. He couldn't stand setbacks. Dr Schroeder will tell you how jumpy and hysterical he became when he was frustrated by some small detail, some little failure.'

'It's not often I hear you quoting Schroeder with approval,' said Jessica wryly.

Dampier acknowledged the thrust with a nod and went on: 'Towards the end the tension was too great for him. He felt that he was on the wrong track. The whole team was on the wrong track — that's how he saw it. They tried to cheer him up, but he wouldn't listen. He killed himself. And the reason that there is no mention of the accident on the file is that we don't like to falsify records.'

Except Western's, she thought sceptically. When you're powerful enough and you want something done, you can falsify as much as you please.

'It wasn't an accident,' said Dampier. 'It was suicide. Quite a few of us know it but we don't talk about it. We never mentioned it to anyone outside, because we wanted to spare the widow and the boy. The Company has looked after both of them very well — and neither of them knows the truth. Perhaps I ought not to have told you, but I feel you should know something about the young man's background. I trust you won't pass this story on to him or to his mother. It's best to let the generally accepted story stand.'

One had to admire the cunning of it. For the general public and fellow workers who had known Richard Marsh only slightly there was the story that it had been an accident. For those less gullible there was a more subtle and doubtless well-authenticated tale of suicide. In this way the more sophisticated, flattered by being in the know, could feel sorry for the man and at the same time indulge in that comfortable contempt with which all good Intersyn types regarded those who couldn't stand the pace.

She wondered if Dampier had any glimmering of that third, deeper truth. She doubted it. If he had been in on the murder he would have been able to advance his own Intersyn career rather more than he had done — or else he would have suffered another unfortunate accident along the way.

Perhaps only two or three men shared

the secret. Perhaps just Partridge and Western. Which left only Partridge now.

It was ingenious. But if David succeeded in what he had set out to do, the secret wouldn't last much longer.

10

Andrew awoke on Sunday morning and stared at sunlight shivering on the wall. He moved his head cautiously on the pillow and looked at his watch. Even that slight movement was enough to wake Jessica. He lay quite still. Although their bodies were not touching he could almost feel the shape of her warmth. Somehow he did not want to turn towards her and look into her face.

It had been an edgy, unsatisfying weekend so far. He couldn't see how it would change now into anything else. He stared at his watch and wondered how long he must allow before he could decently get up, dress, and go out for the papers.

Jess never had newspapers delivered. 'They're such a drug.' she had once told him. 'Headlines screaming at you, and trivialities blown up into significance.' He had thought how odd she was and how wise at the same time. 'I buy them when I feel like it,' she had said, 'and when I don't, I go without. And on Sundays I like to go out in the morning and buy them on the corner anyway.' And he had thought how sensible she was and what an inner tranquillity she had and how original, how very special, how unlike Muriel she was.

Now he lay there and wished that there could be newspapers thumping through the letterbox on to the hall floor. Then he would have an excuse for fetching them and establishing the beginning of a new day. But since they weren't going to come he must wait for the fingers of his watch to move round until they reached the spot when he could reasonably say it was time to go out and get the papers.

A walk in the cold morning would be rather agreeable. A walk on his own. There was a smoky chill in the air that he enjoyed. It would be good to stroll round the corner, collect *The Observer*, *The Sunday Times* and *News of the World* and come back to find Jess getting breakfast ready. She would read *The*

Observer over breakfast. That was the one she always read first. Once they had tossed extracts to and fro aloud, reading and laughing and saying, 'Oh, this is wonderful, you'll never believe this one.' Now he hoped she would read silently.

He was wide awake. She knew it. Her hand crept up and rested on his hip.

Andrew forced a yawn. He twitched as though startled by her touch.

She said: 'Andrew.'

He heaved round in bed to face her. Her breath was hot and sour. He supposed his own was the same. Her eyes were wide open and serious. There had been a time when she kept her eyes half closed like those of a kitten basking in adulation. Now she was staring unwaveringly at him. He looked away, and at once saw her pale shoulder, speckled with a swift rash of goose pimples where the sheet fell away from it. He pulled the sheet up again.

Her lips twitched, her eyes dilated. In the warmth of the bed her hand attacked him suddenly and shamelessly.

'Now, wait,' he spluttered, trying to make it a laugh.

'I don't want to wait.'

'We ought to be getting up.'

'Why?' she said savagely. 'It's early. We're not going anywhere.'

Her fingernails and her warmth and her anger lashed him on. His desire grew at the same pace as his resentment against her. He buried his head in her shoulder and tried to annihilate her: but it was not Jess, it was someone else, someone he had not yet encountered — he was loving a woman who did not yet exist.

Jess rose against him as usual, at the moment he could always calculate — the moment he planned for both of them. In the last moment he drew his head back and looked at her. Now was when she closed her eyes, now the time when she snorted in that frightening paroxysm of hers.

But she made hardly any sound, and she was looking at him with those coldly questioning eyes. Silently she said: Well . . . is this all . . . just this, nothing more?

When they had drawn apart again they lay there for some minutes in silence. It was as though she knew the exact moment when he began to wonder again whether he might reasonably get out of bed now.

She said: 'Well, that wasn't much, was it?'

'It can't be good every time,' he said.

'It never is good now, is it?'

He drew a deep breath. For some reason he groped for her hand and held it tight. She responded. It was a firm, incongruously friendly clasp.

'Jess . . .'

'It's over,' she said.

'No, don't say that.' But he spoke very formally, knowing what he was doing, hearing every inflection as false and knowing that he meant her to hear the same. 'We've both had a pretty trying time,' he said.

'I don't want you to come here again,' said Jessica.

He was conscious of a great relief, flooding over him. And in the flood were splinters of protest. It wasn't up to her to decide when the thing was over. In any case it wasn't over yet. He wouldn't have come here and she wouldn't have wanted him to come if it had all died. But the relief washed warmly over him and he already knew what was going to happen. They would get up and he would fetch the papers and they would have breakfast and there would be sporadic bursts of rather too offhanded conversation. She would not be as interested as she claimed to be in Kenneth Tynan's review; and he would not find the story of the Jamaican under the bed as funny as he made out. They would go for a walk and have a drink in the usual pub, and the more eagerly they talked the more certain it would be that this was indeed the last time. Jessica might cry. He might push his plate away while they were having their belated lunch (not before the pub closed) and say that it was ridiculous, that they couldn't just finish like this. But he knew that this afternoon he would leave this flat and never come back.

The weight would be lifted. The strain would ease. He would be free from

Jessica's demands and from the guilt that her reproaches, spoken or unspoken, caused him.

He would be left with the drabness of life with Muriel.

There would be somebody else. He knew this. He didn't know who it would be but he knew it would happen. Faceless, silent and disembodied as she was at the moment, he already felt a tingle of anticipation. He would start all over again. He knew what it would be like. It came back to him — the pleasure of those first few weeks when you were receptive, when someone appeared, when you were obsessed by some woman's face and voice and the promise of her body. There was nothing to be done about it now: you didn't go out looking for someone, it never worked like that, but when you were in this mood someone always came along.

And this time, this next time, he would organise it better. He would find someone like himself who would take it seriously and passionately yet without commitments on either side. That had to be made clear from the start. If both of you knew where you stood, you could both be happy and relaxed.

That was how he had meant it to be with Jess.

Next time it would work. Next time he would have it all organised.

He said: 'We ought to be thinking of getting up.'

★　★　★

When he had gone, late on Sunday afternoon, Jessica sat by the window and read all the bits of the Sunday papers which she normally neglected. She went through the editorials and the political notes and an article about what was wrong with Ireland, feeling sure that she had read this article before; but it was probable that what was wrong with Ireland now was what had always been wrong with Ireland, so of course all newspaper articles on the subject would be the same. She read the financial columns. There was a mention of Intersyn. A good employee would memorise it and quote a few lines tomorrow just to show willing.

Andrew had gone.

She could do what she liked, go to bed when she liked, meet anyone she liked, go to parties and let her imagination roam instead of keeping it on a tight rein.

She wondered if she would be asked to any parties. It was a long time since she had last accepted an invitation.

Andrew had gone. He had left before — several times — but neither of them had believed in the parting. It had never been serious before. This time she knew he would not come back.

Her mind and body felt empty and sick and tired. She was glad to be alone and she hated him because she was alone.

She wondered what David was doing this weekend and why he hadn't said a word to her.

The telephone rang. It was too much of a coincidence. All she had to do was think of David and there he was, ringing. It was too pat, too funny.

She lifted the receiver. 'David.' She was

so sure that it would be him.

'Vincent 5155?' said the hard woman's voice.

'Yes,' she said. 'Yes, that's right.'

'I have a call for you.'

There was a sequence of clicks and whistles, a faint far-off sighing, and voices that whispered in earnest but unintelligible conversation along some phantom wire. Then there was a clatter in her ear, and, 'Go ahead, please.'

A voice she knew but couldn't identify said: 'Miss Rogers?'

'Yes.'

'Dr Schroeder here.'

'Oh. Dr Schroeder.' She could find nothing else to say to him, late on Sunday afternoon.

'Can you tell me where Mr Dampier is?'

His accent, which she never noticed when they met, was thick and almost comic on the telephone. It made the question sound ridiculous.

'Mr Dampier?' she said. 'I suppose he's at home.'

'No,' said Dr Schroeder reproachfully,

as though she were somehow to blame, somehow negligent, 'he is not at home. I have tried several times. Mrs Dampier has not seen him. It took me a great deal of trouble to find your number.'

'Not seen him?' said Jessica. 'You mean he's left? I mean, he's gone to the hotel . . . '

'Apparently not. We thought you might be able to tell us where he was.'

'I'm afraid I can't.'

'That is a pity.'

Jessica said: 'Is something wrong?'

'It is very strange. Very strange.'

'What is?'

'I think I must tell you that there has been a burglary at Belby.'

Jessica could think of nothing to say. Then she was afraid that her silence would be misinterpreted. She ought at least to express surprise.

'What have they taken?' she ventured. 'A few centrifuges?'

Schroeder breathed disapproval. 'Documents have been taken from our confidential files. The cabinets were opened by someone who knew his way around. It was no ordinary burglary.'

Sickeningly Jessica thought of David. He was so determined to find evidence of his father's murder and of the reasons for it. But David had been on the train with those of them who came back to London. And he didn't know his way around Belby all that well.

Schroeder said: 'You are sure you have no idea where Mr Dampier is?'

'None,' said Jessica.

'Mr Partridge is on his way to London. He will speak to members of the Course tomorrow morning. I am following by the early morning train. I shall be here until midnight in case some word comes through. If Mr Dampier gets in touch with you, will you please let me know?'

'I'll get him to ring you.'

'Please do. And so that there is no mistake, will you also telephone to let us know?'

'Will that be necessary?' asked Jessica stiffly. 'If Mr Dampier rings you — '

'Just to be sure,' said Schroeder, 'let us also hear from you.'

Jessica rang off. The newspapers lay

scattered between the bedroom and the sitting room. She picked up one of them and carried it into the lavatory. But it was impossible to concentrate on garish headlines when the truth was so much more garish. The truth . . . whatever that might be.

Perhaps she ought to go in to the hotel this evening. News might come through there. Dampier might appear there. She could imagine how his lip would curl when he heard of the panic there had been, and how gleefully he would attack Schroeder if he learnt that there had been even the faintest implication of his being involved.

Someone, Schroeder had said, who knew his way around . . .

The telephone began to ring again. Jessica hurried out to lift the receiver before it stopped. She forced herself to give her number calmly, and waited to see who it would be, what news there would be.

There was silence, but she knew that there was somebody at the other end of the line.

'Hello?' she said. 'Yes?'

Still there was only the faint singing along the line and the sound of what must be breathing.

'Who is it?' she said. She was going to speak David's name, then Mr Dampier's — but was suddenly afraid to name anyone at all, not knowing what it might lead to.

At the other end the receiver was gently replaced.

Jessica turned away from the phone. It could have been some crank. It wouldn't have been the first time. Now and then you got the husky voices asking for a fictitious Mary or Eleanor or Susie, and then the sad little obscenities; and occasionally, as now, only the menacing silence. The silence was worse than the smut: even when you knew the poor creature would never come closer to you than that distant telephone, you felt needled by that unspoken lust, and scared of the pressure building up within that perverted mind and body.

Again the ringing started. Jessica snatched up the receiver and said:

'Now look here . . . '

'Miss Rogers?'

'Oh,' said Jessica. 'Oh, yes. Who is that?'

'Margery Dampier here.'

'Oh, Mrs Dampier.'

'Is my husband there?'

Jessica had met Dampier's wife twice. She was a shrewish yet somehow harmless little creature, with a face that must once have been sharply pretty but was now merely bony. At the moment she sounded as though she would like to bite.

Jessica said, 'No, he's not.'

'I see.'

'Dr Schroeder has already been on to me,' said Jessica. 'I believe he's already spoken to you.'

'Yes, he has. Miss Rogers, what is happening? He wouldn't tell me anything. My husband hasn't been home, and they say he's not at the hotel, and *you* don't know where he is — and they sound very odd at Belby. Miss Rogers, it's very upsetting.'

'I'm sure it is.' Jessica tried to sound comforting. 'But there'll be some simple explanation. Mr Dampier must have made some arrangement to call in on friends on his way back to London, or something like that.'

'Without telling me? Without telling you?'

'He must have forgotten. He has a lot of things on his mind.'

'Has he?' said Mrs Dampier quickly. 'What things?'

'Oh, work, of course. You've probably heard how upset we all were about the accident at Belby — '

'I read about it in the papers.'

Jessica sidestepped the obvious implication here. She said: 'I'm sure everything is all right, Mrs Dampier. I expect Mr Dampier will be getting in touch with you any minute now. And' — remembering Schroeder's appeal — 'I'd be awfully grateful if you'd let me know when he does show up. I'd like to have a word with him.'

'And he's not with you?' Mrs Dampier made a last attempt.

'No,' said Jessica, 'he's not with me.'

Having replaced the receiver once more

she wasted no time. She began to pack her bag. She might just as well be at the hotel as here. There was going to be no peace at home this evening.

The next time a bell rang she moved instinctively towards the telephone. There was a lull, the bell rang again, and she realised that it came from the front door.

It might be Andrew back. She felt a rush of hope, cancelled out by immediate resentment. She didn't want it to be Andrew. If he had come ten minutes later, she would have been out of the flat. Let it not be Andrew.

She went to the door.

11

First thing on Monday morning Partridge was driven to the Intersyn building in a Bentley supplied for his use by Head Office Transport Section (Senior Executives, Grade I, Metropolitan Area, chargeable A/c 224/Dir/Lond.). He was joined on the Directors' floor by two of his London colleagues, talked decisively to them for five minutes, and then joined Dr Schroeder ten floors down. Together he and Schroeder went into the room where the Course members were assembled like a class of delinquents due for a dressing-down.

Andrew waited for Jessica to come in. He had heard odd rumours about Dampier and Belby and hoped he could get a private word with Jess during the morning.

She did not appear. Schroeder closed the door deferentially behind Partridge, and there was still no sign of Jessica.

Partridge stood a few inches from the

edge of the lecturer's usual table. He stuck his hands in his pockets and shoved his head forward. He was a skilled inquisitor, sure of his own power, and he intended to have a confession.

He said: 'Everybody here?'

'Mr Dampier has not yet shown up,' said Schroeder, 'and Miss Rogers seems to be late.'

'Anybody else missing?'

Heads turned. Gerald Hornbrook said quietly: 'Young Marsh doesn't appear to be with us this morning.'

Partridge glared at the wall clock. One felt that David Marsh would be made to stand in the corner when he arrived. Miss Rogers, as a member of the staff, would presumably merit a severe reprimand.

They were probably in bed together, thought Andrew sourly. They must have overslept. Perhaps they were having a late breakfast and giggling about the constructions that might be put on their absence. He wondered how long it had taken after he left Jess yesterday — how long before she telephoned Marsh, or before he telephoned her. From one man to another . . . as quickly as that. He was well rid of her.

Had she cried when he left? Had she been wretched? How bad had it been for her?

Andrew pushed the unwelcome thoughts out of his mind and concentrated on what Partridge was saying.

'I can't waste time waiting. I'll begin. The police will be here shortly and I want to talk to you before they arrive. We agreed that they should come at eleven o'clock. They will want to ask you questions. Each one of you will be interrogated. I want you to be quite frank with the police. We trust that none of you has anything to hide. But if he has, I think it would be best to let me know about it now.'

There was a buzz of curiosity from those who had not yet heard the rumours. The others tried to look knowing. Partridge said: 'On Saturday night or the small hours of Sunday morning a burglar ransacked confidential files in the offices at Belby. It was someone who must have had a good working knowledge of the plant and the various buildings. Whatever he was looking for, he had a good idea of where it would be. It may have been one of our own staff up there, but we think this unlikely. The police have found a number of fingerprints which may belong to normal users of the files or to someone else. In due course they will probably want to check on these.'

What, thought Andrew: no existing records? Even Intersyn hadn't got that far . . . yet.

'In addition' — Partridge slowed and looked even more brutal — 'the police are not happy about the circumstances in which Philip Western met his death. The plastic in which Western was embedded is being chipped away by various processes, and quite apart from the distortion of the body from heat and pressure there are marks which seem to indicate violence. It's not for me to make any pronouncements on this at the moment — but if this fits in any way with the theft of the papers, I'll find out about it. I promise you that: I'll find out. If any of you has any help to offer, no matter how small,

I'd like to hear from him.'

His eyes picked out the Course members one by one, saying: Confess . . . repent . . . talk . . . *tell me.*

There was a stricken silence.

Schroeder broke it. 'None of you can help Mr Partridge at all?'

Andrew tried to imagine any one of them putting up his hand and saying, 'Please, sir, it was me, I'm sorry.'

Partridge eased himself back a few steps and perched on the edge of the table. It was an informal posture but he looked as dangerous as ever.

Andrew said: 'You believe there's some connection between Western's death and this burglary, sir?'

'That's what I said.'

'You have no definite accusation to make against any of us?'

'If I had, I'd make it. I've got one or two ideas, but they don't make sense. They don't fit. I want to find a way of making them fit.'

Andrew said: 'If I might make a suggestion . . . '

'I want information,' said Partridge,

'not suggestions.'

It would be politic to stop right there. But Andrew was suddenly impatient. You would get nowhere on this Course or in anything else to do with the Company if you didn't assert yourself. He said:

'We might get information by using some of the techniques we've learnt on this Course.'

Schroeder chuckled in a startling falsetto, anticipating what Andrew was about to say. Partridge scowled. 'I don't follow.'

'We've tackled complicated problems in brainstorm sessions,' said Andrew. 'Provided with a few basic facts, we have had to shape them into a pattern. We've had to give them coherence. While we're waiting for the police, why not do the same thing? Let's see what facts we've got, and analyse them. If we can prepare a comprehensive marketing campaign in a matter of hours, surely we can solve the mystery of a theft and a possible murder if we put our minds to it? Such highly skilled minds,' he added provocatively.

Partridge stared at him. Andrew waited

for the blow to fall. Then Partridge said:

'Bloody good idea.'

Schroeder nodded sycophantically, but there was also a genuine scientific enthusiasm in his face.

'Go ahead,' said Partridge. He slid away from the table and indicated that Andrew should take his place. 'You're in charge. We don't have a great deal of time. Get cracking.'

Andrew went out before the class. He had no chance to regret his brashness. Already they were waiting attentively for him to begin.

Schroeder made for a vacant chair. As he sat down he said: 'Of course, by taking charge like this, Mr Flint may be diverting suspicion from himself. He is in a position to organise the discussion exactly as he wants it. As soon as it approaches dangerous territory he can divert it.'

Andrew hit back fast. 'I'll rely on you to keep it right on course, Dr Schroeder. Tell me as soon as you see me wavering. And have you any theories of your own about the theft — or about the murder?'

'Murder,' said Schroeder reflectively. 'There are basically only two kinds of murder. There's the impulsive one, usually carried out with the aid of a bread knife or the nearest heavy object. And there's the calculated type. The latter is rare. It is even more rare that it should be carried out by anyone as a result of a fit of anger. Once the anger has gone, the impulse to kill has gone — with most of us, anyway. To plan a murder requires a particular kind of fanatical patience — a ruthlessness, an ability to convince oneself that the removal of a certain obstacle to one's comfort or even to one's career is not merely justifiable but is a good thing for mankind in general.'

'Generalisations aside,' said Andrew, 'what do you think about this particular case? Where were you, Dr Schroeder, when Philip Western died? Your office is only a few yards away from the spot, I seem to remember.'

'I was not in my office. I was in the Control Room at the time.'

'You have witnesses for that?'

'Yes,' said Schroeder: 'two assistants —

and Miss Rogers, who had come to see me about some timetable changes favoured by Mr Dampier.'

'Neither Miss Rogers nor Mr Dampier is here to confirm this.'

'No,' agreed Schroeder, unperturbed. 'But the two assistants at Belby have not vanished. I can give you their names if you wish.'

'And the theft?'

'The theft was carried out at night. I was not on duty. Nobody goes to the records section at night, as a rule.'

'But if you had wanted to go there and find something, you'd have known where to look for it? You have the necessary keys?'

'I have the keys that are necessary for my own job.'

'And you know where others are kept?'

'In an emergency, I would know where to find them,' Schroeder agreed.

'And other people at Belby would also know?'

Partridge intervened. 'Only three or four members of the executive are allowed access to all the keys,' he said.

'But plenty of others know where they are. A burglar who knew exactly where to look and who knew what times staff came on and off duty, and where they were likely to be at any given time, could help himself to any documents he wanted. But few of them would be intelligible to anyone outside our own organisation.'

'Nevertheless,' said Andrew, 'someone who was disloyal — maybe someone who was dissatisfied with his job or his prospect of promotion — might be able to pass some useful information to a competitor if it was made worth his while?'

'It could be done. But it could be done a lot more tidily, without drawing attention to it. There was a hell of a mess in the office — drawers tipped over, paper all over the place, cupboards ransacked and left in a shambles. Whoever this was, he didn't cover his tracks.'

'And you don't know yet what he has taken?' said Andrew. 'Or . . . do you?'

'One or two items are definitely missing. We're waiting until the whole lot has been tidied up before we can be sure of others.'

'Anything of value?'

Partridge hesitated, then said: 'Nothing. Nothing of any real significance — so far as we can tell.'

'An interesting point,' said Schroeder, 'is that one man who frequently boasted of knowing the place inside out and of being able to circumvent all our security precautions is not here today. He ought to be here.'

Everyone in the room sat very still.

Andrew said: 'All right. Where was Mr Dampier at the time of the theft?'

'That is what we would like to know. He was supposed to have come back to London, but nobody has seen him. His wife does not know where he is: he was not at home during the weekend. He did not go to the hotel. And his secretary denied all knowledge of him.'

'His secretary?' Andrew wondered when they had been in touch with Jessica; whether they were keeping her out of the room for some sly reason of their own.

'I spoke to her myself yesterday afternoon.'

'And where is she now?' demanded Partridge irascibly.

'I don't know,' said Schroeder.

Andrew was tempted to display his superior knowledge by telling them where Jess was. If she wasn't being kept incommunicado at their orders, there was surely little doubt of where she was — or, at least, who she was with.

Instead, he went on: 'And where was Mr Dampier at the time of Western's death?'

Schroeder's puffy face seemed to swell, malignant in its spiteful glee. 'I am afraid I cannot tell you that. It was very odd. There was a dispute between Mr Dampier and myself over the organisation of the timetable, and at such times Mr Dampier makes a point of seeing me personally. He likes to put his views across forcibly — face to face. But on this occasion he sent Miss Rogers. What he did while Miss Rogers was away, I do not know.'

'But I do,' said Partridge.

They turned towards him. Schroeder looked hurt. He had built up a nice aura of suspense and did not want it spoilt.

'Dampier was with me,' said Partridge. 'He was talking to me about a personal matter.'

That was that. Partridge's tone brooked no further discussion. But Andrew, launched on the tide, was in no mood for compromise. With a surprising lack of trepidation he heard himself saying:

'I'm sorry, Mr Partridge, but if we're to continue this enquiry we need all the facts.'

Partridge went very red. 'Even in your brainstorm sessions,' he snorted, 'you can't have *all* the facts.'

'But we ought to have them. Planning a marketing campaign when there are too many unknown quantities is a risky business. Investigating a crime — two crimes — when information is consciously withheld is just as risky. If we're going to take it seriously, we want all the details we can get. Unless the matter is very confidential, sir, I think you ought to tell us why Mr Dampier came to see you.'

Again there was a breathless pause. Then the indignation ebbed from Partridge's face, and he grinned crookedly.

'All right, Flint. I'll play. Dampier came to see me because someone had put it into his head that he was being watched. Thought there was someone on the Course keeping tabs on him and preparing evidence against him.'

The suppressed gasp from the class was eerily, faintly audible.

'And was there?' asked Andrew.

'Of course there wasn't. He wanted my personal assurance that he was not marked down for redundancy and that we were not trying to catch him out in any way. He got it.'

'Did he have any theory about who it was who was watching him — supposed to be watching him, that is?'

'Yes. He thought it was Western.'

'But he was with you when Western was killed.'

'That's right.'

Andrew indulged in a moment of wild speculation as to whether Partridge and Dampier had somehow been working together, covering up for each other — or whether Dampier had found something with which he could blackmail Partridge, and Partridge had therefore disposed of him. But even in his present mood of abandonment Andrew realised it was best not to put such speculations into words. Not yet. All he said was:

'Why should anyone have found it necessary to kill Western? What did he know — or what did he see?'

Hornbrook said quietly: 'We are now taking it for granted that Western was murdered, I observe.'

There was a tap at the door. A timid girl looked in, and grew even more frightened as faces turned towards her. She took a few steps towards Andrew, then blinked and looked round for someone whose authority she recognised.

Partridge snapped: 'What is it?'

'Oh. Er, it's a message, sir. From Mr — er — Mr Marsh.'

'Marsh? Where the devil is he?'

'It was a phone call, sir. He wanted to say that he's had a breakdown driving in from Maidenhead. He's very sorry, sir, but he thought he ought to ring up and say what had happened, and he'll be in as soon as he can, sir.'

'Thank you.' It was a curt dismissal. The girl scurried out.

'I shall be interested,' said Schroeder drily and significantly, 'to hear what Mr Marsh has to say for himself when he gets here. Perhaps' — he smiled at Andrew — 'Mr Flint will have some questions ready for him.'

The brief lull while the girl was speaking had given other members of the Course time for thought. They realised that Andrew had seized the initiative — even, perhaps, that this whole thing was rigged, was all part of the Course itself. It was time they asserted themselves. Three men began to speak at once, and all stopped at once in confusion. Before they could recover, Ames got a word in. Clearly and precisely he said:

'Would it not be a good idea to proceed step by step? I suggest that very quickly we establish where each one of us was at the time of Western's death, and then where each one of us was when the theft took place. It should be possible to eliminate a large number of suspects in a very short time.'

'Do that,' Partridge approved.

Andrew took him up on this without hesitation. He said: 'Mr Crowther — where were you when Western died?'

'Me?' Crowther groped immediately in his pocket for his pipe and brought it out as though it were a defensive weapon. 'Now, wait a minute — '

'Answer him,' said Partridge.

Crowther stuck the empty pipe between his teeth and sucked at it as he spoke.

'I was out,' he said. 'I'd gone out into the town for a while.'

'Why?'

'Because I felt like it.'

'Can anyone confirm your story?'

'I don't suppose so. I just felt like a walk. I used to work there, and I went out to see what the old place was like.'

'Which way did you go out?' Andrew asked.

'What do you mean?'

'Did you go out of the main gate?'

'What other way would I go out?'

271

Andrew said: 'On one occasion we . . . I saw you making use of a side entrance — the entrance closest to the building in which Western was killed. You know your way about the place pretty well, Mr Crowther.'

Crowther's heavy features lost their bluff brightness and settled into sullenness. He did not reply.

'Did you have any reason for getting Western out of the way?' said Andrew.

'No.'

'He didn't perhaps intercept you on one of your mysterious walks — on your way in, or out?'

'No,' said Crowther, 'he didn't.'

'But you are not prepared to tell us where you went and why?'

'I've told you.'

'Did you regard Western as a serious rival on the Course, one who must be got out of the way? Or' — Andrew was enjoying the inquisition, enjoying the liberty he had been given to strike out, to say what he chose, to make them jump — 'did *you* think you were being watched? Was there some reason — something to do with your past in Belby — to make you afraid of being watched?'

'You're a nosy bastard, aren't you,' said Crowther flatly.

Schroeder cleared his throat. He did so with relish, announcing that he had something enjoyable to say. 'I cannot provide Mr Crowther with an alibi in the sense that I was with him at the time of the death. As I have already told you, I was with Miss Rogers at that time. But I think I can tell you where he went on these evening strolls of his.'

'Shut up,' said Crowther. 'What's it got to do with you?'

'It should be put on record,' said Schroeder, 'that Mr Crowther not merely spent some of his early days in the factory at Belby, but was in fact a local inhabitant — a local lad, I think they say. When he was young and humble, he married a local girl — '

'This isn't anyone's concern but my own,' raged Crowther.

'Don't be too sure you won't need an alibi,' purred Schroeder. 'Yes . . . Mr Crowther married young. Then he started

273

to rise in the world. He soon found that his wife was . . . how shall I put it? . . . no great asset. She weighed him down when he wanted to climb.'

'Ah've never made any secret about my origins,' said Crowther, his accent thickening. 'Never made any secret about where I come from. You don't find me putting on any side. So that's a libel. That's what it is. A libel.'

'A slander rather than a libel. If it were a slander. But I don't think it is. It's one thing to flaunt a no-nonsense accent — the Scots, Yorkshiremen, and my own countrymen all do very well in industry by preserving just enough of their original inflection to show that they are men of great integrity, quite free from affectation — but one doesn't want to flaunt a wife who is obstinately unsociable, provincial, and unwilling to move away from the semi-detached house which has always been her dream world. So one divorces her — or, rather, makes it worth her while to divorce one. And one marries a more suitable woman. When a rich, well-educated woman with a Roedean voice marries a simple Yorkshireman it makes it clear that he is a man of unsuspected potentialities beneath that rugged exterior, doesn't it? And when he moves on up the ladder, she helps him up.'

'You're going to be sorry for this,' said Crowther.

'Sorry? As sorry as you've been over the years — as guilty as you have felt?' Schroeder shook his head. His tone remained scientific and detached. 'It still makes you uneasy to think about that baffled little woman who never knew what hit her — who gave you your divorce without understanding why it should have happened to her. And you couldn't resist going to see her while you were in Belby, could you? A friendly call . . . to see that she was all right . . . to flagellate yourself, and at the same time to get her to say that she was perfectly happy and it didn't matter at all.'

'You're making all this rubbish up.'

'I don't think so. You carry the past round with you, Mr Crowther — not just in little notes and opinions on your personal record file with the Company, but in your face. And plenty of people in Belby still remember you.'

There was an uncomfortable silence.

Andrew said: 'We've rather got off the point. The second question, Mr Crowther — '

'I'll answer no more questions.'

'Where were you this weekend, when the theft took place?'

'Oh, that,' said Crowther. 'My wife will confirm that I reached home late on Friday night.'

'Your wife?'

'My second wife,' growled Crowther. 'And on Saturday night we had friends in. I played golf on Sunday morning with one of 'em. So that lets me out, doesn't it?'

Andrew had to accept this for the time being. 'Well, who's next?'

'What about yourself?' It was Ames again, his tongue dabbing excitedly against his upper lip.

There was a ripple of laughter. Andrew recognised it as the laughter of approval. 'All right,' he said quickly. 'What about me?'

Ames stood up, fancying himself as a prosecuting counsel, and tweaked at the edges of a non-existent gown. He said:

'Several of us observed considerable antipathy between yourself and the late Philip Western. You are an ambitious man and probably none too scrupulous. Also you have been indulging in — ah — some kind of relationship with Miss Rogers — '

'How the hell . . . what right have you to say that?'

There was a boom of delight from Crowther. 'Now look who's squirming!'

'It is not for me to guess at the exact nature of the relationship,' said Ames primly, 'but certainly there were indications of a warm friendship between you. And Miss Rogers, as permanent secretary for all the Executive Courses, would know a great deal about the layout at Belby. She is used to handling confidential files. She would know how to get at those at Belby, and how to interpret them for you. What did she find out on your behalf, Flint? What information did she give you?'

'Miss Rogers gave me no information whatsoever.'

'Where were you,' said Ames, 'at the time of Western's death?'

There was no danger here. Andrew said: 'I was in the bar, talking to Hornbrook.'

'True,' said Hornbrook, almost with regret.

'And at the time of the theft?'

At the time of the theft. Oh, then I was in bed with Jessica Rogers. Andrew heard the sentence so clearly in his head that he was afraid he might inadvertently have said it aloud. But Ames was staring hopefully at him and waiting.

'Well?' said Ames.

'I was in London. You saw me on the train yourself, when we came down.'

'You could have turned round and gone back.'

If the charges were pressed home he might sooner or later have to answer. That would finish his chances on this Course. There might be laughter and even some envious congratulations. But the fact that he had been to bed with Jessica Rogers

278

would tell against him in the final summing-up. It was ironical: they had kept it so quiet for so long, and now that the affair was ended there was a danger of the whole world hearing about it.

He said: 'I didn't go back.'

'Did you spend the weekend at home? With your wife? Did friends come in — and did you play golf?'

There was no one here with the legal authority to demand an answer. But Andrew knew what a refusal to answer could mean. He was the one who had started this dangerous game, and they would expect him to play according to his own rules. Partridge would certainly hold it against him if he didn't.

He was saved by the door opening.

David Marsh came in.

Partridge said: 'Where have you been?'

'Sorry about this. I decided to drive into town this morning, and had a spot of bother on the way. I hope I haven't missed anything.'

It was hardly an apology. Young Marsh appeared to be laughing to himself. There was a wild gleam in his eye, and the corners of his mouth kept twitching with amusement. Pleased with himself, thought Andrew: full of it, bubbling over with it, no end of a fellow because he's got Jess on the rebound. The two of them, laughing in bed and laughing on their way up this morning, not giving a damn about being late, not giving a damn about anything. It wouldn't last. It would soon wear off. And in the meantime David Marsh would have finished himself so far as Intersyn was concerned.

Andrew wondered how long it would be before Jessica slipped apologetically into the room. She would allow a reasonable length of time to elapse, and then come in with some other glib story. He glanced at the clock. He would time her. And he would let her see that he, at least, knew the truth of the matter.

Schroeder said: 'We are in the middle of a brainstorm session, Mr Marsh.'

'Sorry I've missed it.'

'You have not missed it. It is unusual to allow new entrants in the middle, but in this case I think you can join us without difficulty.' Without waiting to see if

Partridge or Andrew had anything to say, Schroeder gave a brief outline of what had happened. Marsh grinned boyishly throughout. Evidently he found it vastly entertaining.

When Schroeder had finished, Partridge spoke. He said:

'Since you are here, Marsh, you can be the next subject for questioning.'

David Marsh smiled. 'What about yourself, Mr Partridge?'

It was the question Andrew had wanted but not dared to ask. Now this young fool, bumptious with the memory of Jess's responsive body, was stamping cheerfully on.

'Don't be so bloody impertinent,' said Partridge.

'Since Western was one of your own men — '

'That's enough, Marsh. I don't have to answer to you.'

'Oh, yes, you do.' David Marsh was deadly behind his smile. 'You've got a lot to answer for to me.' He strolled towards Partridge and stood above him, languid yet purposeful. 'Western was one of your protégés. He was on this Course because you put him on it. It could be that he found something he ought not to have found — something which embarrassed you.' The young man tossed this off as though he did not take it seriously but wanted to goad Partridge into some other admission. 'You might have decided it was necessary to get rid of him. And in order to remove incriminating documents from the files, you might have staged a deliberately clumsy burglary, to draw suspicion away from yourself.'

'Rubbish.'

'I suppose it is,' said Marsh. His recklessness and volatility were disquieting. 'All the same, something incriminating *did* disappear from those files, didn't it? Something you wouldn't want other people to see.'

Partridge unexpectedly relaxed. He sat back with something amounting almost to satisfaction, tinged with an odd sadness. He said:

'So it was you. I thought it must be.'

David Marsh did not reply at once. He looked down reflectively at Partridge. He might have been debating where to plunge the knife in.

Andrew glanced at the door. It must surely open soon. It was time Jess appeared. Was she going to stay in her office all day, pretending to be ignorant of everything that was going on?

Marsh said quietly: 'What was Western doing on the Course, Mr Partridge? Will you tell the class that?'

'Dampier had the idea that Western was watching someone,' contributed Blackwell from the back row, nervous but eager.

'Who was he watching?'

Partridge returned Marsh's steady gaze and said: 'He was watching you.'

'Why?'

'Because we were afraid you would do something stupid. We wanted to protect the Company and certain of its employees against any misguided behaviour on your part.'

'You wanted to protect yourself,' said Marsh. 'You wanted to stop me getting too close to the truth.'

'We didn't want a scene,' said Partridge doggedly. 'We didn't want a scandal.'

'But you're going to get one. You do realise that now, don't you?'

'Yes,' said Partridge, 'I realise that.'

David Marsh said: 'Will you tell our friends here why you were so horrified when you learnt I was on the Course — why you set one of your top men to spy on me — why you're so worried about the things that may be missing from Belby? Tell them particularly about my father's notebook.'

'You murdered Western,' said Partridge; 'and you ransacked our files. Do you deny that?'

'I took certain interesting items from your files,' said Marsh equably. 'Would you like me to tell the class what they were?'

Partridge stood up abruptly. His sheer physical presence was enough to make the younger man step back a few paces. Partridge came on like a bulldog, his head down, his shoulders swinging meatily.

'How did you find out about those files? Who told you where things were — who let you in?'

'Those are minor questions. Don't try

to obscure the issue. The important thing is what I found there — what my father wrote before he was killed. Before he was killed, Mr Partridge.'

There was a babble of voices in the room. All the self-restraint in the world wouldn't hold it in. Marsh and Partridge confronted each other across the bobbing heads and the startled, upturned faces.

Andrew stepped into the middle of the tumult. He put one hand on David Marsh's shoulder and spun him round. There was one person who could have given Marsh the information he needed to locate those files — a person for whom Andrew had provided an alibi on the night of the actual theft if she should ever need it, but who had now disappeared. He didn't know why she had disappeared, but he was frightened.

He said: 'Where's Jess?'

Marsh stared blankly at him.

'Yes,' said Partridge. 'Where's Miss Rogers?'

He and Andrew had the young man pinned between them. He seemed unconcerned. 'I'm sorry, but I really can't help you.' He was still looking at Andrew and his cheek muscles were flickering in that crazy smile. 'I had the impression she was spending the weekend with you.'

A facetious voice rose from the hubbub. 'Maybe Miss Rogers has run off with Mr Dampier. It's a bit of a coincidence, both of them being missing, isn't it?'

The laughter was uncertain. Marsh's smile, however, broadened. He said: 'An interesting line of thought. What do you think, Mr Partridge? Mr Dampier and Miss Rogers — they must know an awful lot between them. Rather uncomfortable for you, perhaps?'

'You murdered Western,' said Partridge again.

'Can you think of any good reason why I should have murdered Mr Western? I'd have preferred him to live, to appear as a witness . . . to be under oath, when I bring my case against Intersyn. And against you in particular, Mr Partridge. As it is, I now have what will probably be called Exhibit A — my father's notebook.'

Andrew saw the two faces close to him:

the young fanatical face and the tight, grim, remorseless face of Partridge.

The idea of Dampier and Jess going off together was absurd. But where were they? Not that he gave a damn about Dampier. But that neighing ninny had been right: it was a bit of a coincidence.

David Marsh said: 'If you'll allow me room to breathe, I'll tell you about what you're pleased to call the theft from Belby. Though how it can be theft, when you had no business to be holding on to somebody else's property in the first place . . . ' He waited until the two men had stepped back and allowed him to make his way to the front of the class once more. 'I'll tell you what happened,' he said. 'Right from the beginning. I'll tell you what really happened.'

Andrew waited for the door to open, for Jess to come in, for her to appear in the middle of a sentence. But she did not come. Where was she?

12

Jessica said: 'Don't you see that it's all your doing? It's been your fault from a long way back. You must have known it would come to something like this in the end.'

'No.' The appalled whisper rustled round the cellar like a mouse scurrying within the walls.

A naked forty-watt bulb hung from the ceiling. The cellar was bare but not too cold. There was a bench against one wall, littered with tools which had not been used for a long time. In the faint dust that lay across the bench were the outlines of a chisel and a screwdriver, perfectly etched — tools that had recently been taken away.

And in a corner, darker than the shadows, was the hideous huddled mass they dared not look at.

Jessica pressed herself against the wall and looked up at the tiny grating. It admitted fresh air but allowed nothing out. She had shouted, and no one had answered. At intervals she raised her head and shouted again; and still there was no reply, no help.

There were some substantial-looking implements on the bench. She had studied them all and conceived splendidly dramatic plans for escape — plans involving shorting the power supply, setting the house on fire and banking on the fire brigade arriving on time, or using a screwdriver on the door, getting the lock away, somehow removing the hinges. It would all have looked fine in a film and it was all impracticable.

Every now and then her thwarted energy burst out in a rage of accusation.

'You wanted something done . . . but you didn't want to hear how it was carried out, did you? You just didn't want to know. And now you know.'

Then they both looked at the horror in the corner and shivered and looked away. They had seen it all too clearly this morning.

It seemed a lifetime since that ring at

her doorbell. She had opened the door to find David there. He was smiling. He was unable to stop smiling: triumph was written all over his face. He kissed her and then slapped her lightly several times on the shoulder — the slap he might have given an old school friend who would understand that it meant something big, something special, something almost too big to be told.

'David.'

She stood back to let him in but he still stood outside.

He said: 'I hoped you'd be in. I'd like you to come down and spend the rest of the day with us. And stay the night. We can drive in early tomorrow morning and report for duty. Coming?' He was already catching her arm and drawing her boisterously out on to the landing, where the iron-framed lift waited.

'But . . . ' She floundered. She had no excuse for not going with him, but no immediate reason for going. 'I'm not ready.'

'Aren't you?' He laughed and walked past her, and saw her bag already packed.

'You can soon get ready.'

'Why didn't you call me first?'

He hesitated. A question formed in her mind — the silence on the telephone, the gentle replacing of the receiver — but before she could utter it he said: 'Here's your case. On the way to the hotel? But you don't want to stay in that dismal dump. We'll be there long enough, goodness knows. Or will we? Depends on tomorrow morning.'

'What do you mean?' she asked.

'Come on,' he said. 'I had to drive into town. I've got the car here. We can be home in thirty minutes, or thereabouts. Mother'd love to see you.'

She tried to argue and realised that he was not listening. She thought about Dampier and about the messages that might reach the hotel. They would try to get in touch with her. They would be cross if she wasn't there, even if they had nothing to report. It was her job: she was a sponge, a shock-absorber, a buffer, a soothing murmur, producing comforting platitudes to order.

'I ought to go to the hotel,' she said. 'A

lot of them will be checking in tonight.'

'Let them.' David picked up her bag and walked out. She found that she was following him. 'After all,' he said, 'you may not be working for Intersyn that much longer.'

He was so confident that she was incapable of argument. It was all too soon — too soon after Andrew, too soon to think of anything or of anybody else — but his exuberance was infectious. She slammed the door behind her and followed him downstairs and out to his car.

He put her case on the back seat and opened the front door for her with a flourish.

They went out of London fast. He drove as he had certainly not driven on that previous occasion when they toured decorously around the Maidenhead area. He was humming to himself, and he used the car as a partner in a dance.

Jessica said: 'David . . . we don't want to get killed. At least, I don't.'

'No,' he agreed. 'Not before tomorrow morning. Not before I've told them.'

'Told them what?'

He laughed. She looked at him and he turned to look full at her. The car jolted. He glanced back at the road as though daring it to offer any opposition. Headlights were just being switched on in the misty twilight. The uncertain light cast strange shadows down David's face. In a moment of brightness Jessica realised how red and tired his eyes were. Her throat was dry as she said:

'You've driven a long way today.'

'That's right.'

'You didn't drive in from Maidenhead to pick me up. You . . . you've been up to Belby. David — it was you.'

'Tomorrow morning you must watch their faces,' he said. 'I won't be able to concentrate on all of them when I break the news. You must tell me later how they took it.' They went round a roundabout with a faint wail of tyres. 'Mother will be so pleased. I wanted you to be there when I told her. I want you both to be in on it. Things are going to be so different from now on.'

'What did you find?' she demanded.

'And how did you know where to look?'

He shook his head as though brushing off an importunate child.

'Later,' he said. 'Later, when I can tell you both.'

She wanted to tell him to stop. She wanted to get out and discuss things calmly and clear her head and think things out calmly. But he drove on. He did not speak again until they were in the house.

Mrs Marsh kissed him and looked past him at Jessica, questioning her right to be here.

'You must be worn out, Davy. Whatever have you been up to all this time?'

'I rang you — '

'Made no sense to me. No sense at all. Now come on, let me take your coat. You go right in and sit down.'

She plucked at his coat sleeves. Her voice was querulous and her eyes adoring.

David said: 'I've done it.'

'Whatever that may be, I expect it'll wait until we all sit down.'

'I've proved it. I've got Father's notebook.'

Mrs Marsh's shoulders had bowed with the weight of the coat. Now she stood leaning forward, stooped, stricken. Jessica moved forward to help her with the coat. Mrs Marsh straightened up, hung the coat on a hook, and turned back to her son.

'I knew you'd find out someday, somehow,' she said.

The two of them went into the sitting room. Jessica followed, feeling that she was trespassing. She would not have been surprised if they had bowed to the picture of Mr Marsh.

'Now,' said Mrs Marsh.

The two women sat down. David stood before the mantelpiece with his back to his father. He said:

'When we left Belby I came down with the others, and then I came home.' His mother nodded at Jessica to intimate that this preamble was for her benefit. 'Then I got the car out and drove back to Belby on Saturday. I found all the development files of the project my father was working on. His notebook was there. And there are things on the final pages that they'll have difficulty in explaining away. I don't understand the formulae — they're far ahead of anything I've ever touched — but I expect some good Intersyn men will understand them. Understand them too well. I fancy!'

Mrs Marsh nodded proudly.

Jessica said: 'David, don't you realise what you've done?'

'I've reclaimed what belongs to us.'

'You've broken into Intersyn property, and you've stolen from confidential files.'

'I was sure you didn't understand my boy,' said Mrs Marsh. 'Right from the start I was sure of it.'

'Mother — '

'What does she know about it? What does she know of the years we've waited, the years we've longed to show up the truth?'

'It's all right, Jess,' said David gently. 'It's quite a day for us. You do understand that, don't you? And I know how you feel about breaking in and stealing. But do you think I wanted to do things that way? It's just that there was no other way of finding out. They weren't going to hand over the truth of their own free will.'

'Who stole things in the first place, anyway?' Mrs Marsh demanded fiercely. 'Who stole Mr Marsh's ideas, his years of work, his notebook — everything?'

'His notebook.' David echoed the words. Then he went out of the room and they heard him open the back door and go out. Mrs Marsh stared at Jessica in silent hostility.

When David returned he held out a small black notebook. His mother touched it with the tips of her fingers then shook her head reverently.

'I wouldn't understand a thing.'

David held the book out to Jessica. She opened it. The figures, all written in a neat, almost constricted style, meant nothing to her. She felt that the writing deteriorated towards the end of the book: some lines were scrawled half-way down a page and then tilted in a drunken swoop; but this must be where excitement had gripped Mr Marsh, when he couldn't get the final revelations down fast enough.

David said: 'Don't worry, Jess. Once they know that this is in my possession they won't be too keen to lay any charges against me. You'll see.'

Then he sat down, put his head back, and closed his eyes. He was exhausted. His mother at once began to fuss over him. He had done too much, he must go to bed at once — all that dashing about, he ought to have known better, she didn't know what he'd get up to next.

But when he opened his eyes again and smiled at her, she nodded a secret, conspiratorial nod at him. 'After all this time,' she whispered. 'After all this time. But I knew you'd do it, son.'

Jessica was sorry she had come. David had said that he wanted her to share in it, but the triumph was his and his mother's. She was excluded. She had all the uneasy tremors of an accessory after the fact without sharing in any of the profits. Then David put out his arm and drew her closer, forcing his mother to accept her as one of the group, as part of the future.

They went to bed early. Jessica lay awake for some time wondering if David would come into the small spare room.

But he would be saving his energy for tomorrow; and probably, too, he would feel that it was blasphemous to make love to her on this night, in his mother's house, in a house haunted by his dead father.

In the morning they were up early. Mrs Marsh insisted that David should have a good breakfast. She wanted him to be strong enough to deal with all that was going to happen today. When she kissed him goodbye it was a long, affectionate leavetaking. Her gallant son was riding out to clear his father's name.

Jessica carried her case round to the back of the car. She snapped open the lid of the boot.

'Not in there!' yelled David suddenly.

The boot was full. Dampier's body had been squashed into the confined space. His head was half concealed by one arm, but enough was visible to show that the face had been hideously scarred by acid burns and knife or chisel wounds. There were long tears in his jacket and trousers, the edges unevenly stuck together by dried blood.

'Oh,' said David close behind her. 'Oh, dear.' He spoke with a touch of gentle reproach. Behind him his mother wailed — a soft, animal cry — and sagged against the door. David leaned past Jessica and slammed down the lid of the boot. Then he took her arm, and she had no strength in her to fight free. 'You weren't meant to see that,' he said, turning her with surprising speed and vigour towards the door and back into the house.

★   ★   ★

Detective Inspector Freeman and his sergeant suggested courteously that the best way to deal with the matter was to interview Course members one by one, and that it would be advisable for the interviewed men not to return to the classroom afterwards. Detective Inspector Freeman was very polite about this but very firm.

Partridge thought the procedure would now be unnecessary. He felt that the two policemen should listen to what this young gentleman here had to say first. They had arrived just in time.

Freeman pointed out that the young man ought to be warned before making any statement.

'Mr Marsh is merely addressing his colleagues on the Course,' said Partridge. 'You are merely here as guests. I am sure you will discover a lot more that way, and save yourselves a lot of time. And at least you can't complain of lack of witnesses. Whatever Mr Marsh may say, he will have difficulty in retracting it afterwards.'

'Very well, sir.'

Partridge said: 'Go on, Mr Marsh.'

David Marsh looked much more at ease than many official lecturers on this Course had done. One would have said that he understood his subject perfectly and was skilled at putting it across.

He told them what had happened. Leaving Belby, going back to Belby, getting in through a side gate, going into the records office at a time when he knew the night duty staff would be in another part of the plant, opening the files with the spare key that was always kept in a certain desk drawer, finding the development files, and above all finding his father's notebook.

He raised his right hand with the notebook in it. There was an oath-taking significance in the gesture.

'Here it is,' he said. 'Here's the truth. It's all written down here, in this book. You'll see who started the whole project. And you'll see who finished it off. Intersyn's money — its prosperity — all the profits that have rolled in over the last few years . . . the beginning is here.' He put the notebook down on the desk in front of a man with heavily black-rimmed glasses. 'Here. This is your line of country. Read those last few pages and tell me what they mean. Tell me . . . tell everybody.'

The man gulped and opened the book.

'Right at the end,' said David Marsh. 'Tell the members of this Course what those formulae mean.'

There was a silence, broken only by the rustle of pages being turned over. The detective inspector and his sergeant, sitting stiffly on chairs at the side of the room, leaned forward as though ready to spring. But nobody was trying to escape; nobody was running away.

Partridge said: 'You do realise, of course — '

'Be quiet,' said David. 'Unless you're afraid to let everyone else hear the truth, that is.'

Partridge said to the detective inspector: 'This man is mad. I hope you'll be able to cope with him.'

'We'll manage, sir.'

'Mad?' said David Marsh. 'Read out what's on those last few pages. Tell them!'

The unhappy man in the front row took off his glasses and breathed on them, then rubbed them with a scrap of papery cloth taken from a small packet. He looked again at the last page, but only briefly, and then shook his head.

He said: 'It's all gibberish. It doesn't mean a thing.'

'You see?' said Partridge.

'You're lying! You're one of *them*! Show it to someone else — someone independent. You know it's not true.'

'The earlier part of the book is

straightforward. A lot of wastage, but even at a glance one can see where it's leading. We're all familiar with the fundamentals by now. But towards the end it rambles off into . . . well, scribblings.'

Detective Inspector Freeman got to his feet. He looked unhappily round the room. He was not sure on whose shoulder his hand ought to fall.

David Marsh let out a high, shrill breath. 'You're covering up. My father did all the work . . . you stole his ideas and killed him . . . and you're all in it. Give me that.'

He snatched the notebook back.

It was Dr Schroeder who came quietly towards him and touched his arm. There was a sad, appealing note in his voice.

'Your father was a great man,' he said. 'He gave a great deal to Intersyn, and we were all proud to work with him. But he was highly strung. He was difficult to get on with at times. And at the end he was . . . unsettled.'

'You're a liar.'

'Seriously unsettled,' said Schroeder gently but firmly.

'You can't trick me. You can't talk me down. You can't hide the truth for ever. Look — any one of you — read this. What about you . . . you . . . ?'

He was staring at Andrew, as though knowing that someone who detested him would nevertheless give an honest answer.

'At the end,' said Partridge brutally, 'Marsh was insane. The diary makes that clear. That was why we held on to it.' He turned towards the police. The sergeant was just getting to his feet. 'Marsh began to get some pretty nasty delusions in the later stages of his work. He got persecution mania. He felt frustrated, he couldn't break through the final problems single-handed, and so he turned against the other men on the project. We were worried about him — but not worried enough, as it turned out later. I'm not denying I feel guilty about Marsh. I do — but not for the reasons his son thinks. I feel guilty because I didn't take him off the project and make sure he got proper medical treatment. We didn't realise he was boiling up quite so fast. The truth of the matter is that Richard Marsh committed suicide.'

David Marsh threw himself at Partridge. Detective Inspector Freeman moved with surprising speed and was suddenly between the two of them. He got a grip on David, and the two of them reeled away across the room.

Partridge was determined to finish. He raised his voice, hectoring yet patently sincere. 'We hid that notebook,' he said, 'because we wanted to protect the widow and son. He was just a boy then. Also there'd have been trouble with insurance, trouble over the widow's right to a Company pension. Maybe we should have destroyed it . . . but' — he grinned sourly — 'in this Company you file everything away. And it wouldn't have stopped young Marsh here building up his fantasies about the wrongs his father suffered at our hands. The book meant everything to him, whether it still existed or not. To anyone else, it means nothing because . . . well, because it literally means nothing.'

David fought against the detective and twisted him towards the wall. The sergeant moved in closer and planted one large hand on David's left elbow. The young man was immobilised for a moment.

Partridge turned to him and said: 'I'm sorry, but it's all true. We're not villains. We didn't steal any of your father's secrets. He wasn't robbed, he wasn't murdered. He was mentally unbalanced and he killed himself.'

David was straining forward now, yelling at him. Andrew watched in horror. He recognised the truth when he saw it yet felt hatred for Partridge, the man who was telling the truth. Then that feeling went under the pressure of another — of fear for Jessica's safety. He tried to speak, but Partridge went on, louder and louder, as though to beat David Marsh to his knees.

'Richard Marsh was unstable,' he said. 'His son has inherited the more dangerous tendencies.'

'It's a lie . . . a lie . . . a lie. You're scared. It was you who put Western up to it — told him the same story — got him to sneer at me, sneer at my father — '

And Andrew, already about to speak, said instinctively: 'So that's why you killed Western?'

'Of course,' said prim, shrewd little Ames gleefully.

They were like angry troops with a wretched captive, each wanting to add a kick; like dogs diving in to tear at the fox.

Andrew said: 'It was you who knocked me out that night in the hotel. Nosing into files right at the start. You soon guessed someone was on your trail. When did you know it was Western? And where were you on the night when Western was killed?'

'I'll tell you where I was.' Still panting, still twisting vainly in the professional grip of the two stony-faced detectives, David Marsh said: 'I went to see Dr Schroeder to get the truth out of him. He was one of them. He knew. He'd made it clear to me that he worked with my father, and he pretended to like him. But I knew. I could see. I went to him, to give him a chance to show that he was sincere . . . or to give himself away. I knew that someone, sooner or later, would give himself away.'

'And . . . ?'

'And he wasn't there.'

'So what did you do?'

'I went away.'

But they all knew now how it must have been. No need for a brainstorm, no need for telepathy. They hardly dared to look at each other, because they knew so much all at once. Western had followed David Marsh, still keeping an eye on him, still acting on Partridge's instructions. And David had suddenly come out of Schroeder's office — perhaps having spent a long time turning over papers cautiously and opening drawers — and had bumped into Western.

Partridge said: 'What did Western say to you?'

'I don't know what you're talking about.'

Western would have reacted contemptuously, thought Andrew, to disguise the fact that he had been caught off balance. If David Marsh had accused him of being a paid spy, he would have retaliated by sneering. Sneering came naturally to

Philip Western. He would have said, in an unguarded moment, that David's father committed suicide.

And David would have thrown him over the rail into the smoothly flowing resin.

Suddenly David Marsh went limp. The detectives had to hold him up. He said: 'He oughtn't to have been there. I didn't want to have anything to do with Western. All I wanted was the notebook — and now I've got it — and you can't hide it any more, you can't pretend it doesn't exist. You all know the truth, however you try to hide it.'

They took him away. Partridge, about to follow, said: 'We'll find out the whole story in the end. But what I'd like to know right now is — how did he find out so much about Belby? How did he know the way in, and where the files were, and where the spare key was kept?'

What Andrew Flint wanted to know was where Jessica was. He was scared that his own question and Partridge's questions were one and the same. And he wasn't sure that he would find Jess alive.

'I didn't mean it to be like this,' whimpered Mrs Marsh.

'No, you didn't mean it,' said Jessica. She knew that she should feel pity for the woman, but she was possessed by a terrible anger against her. 'You fed him with stories about his father, stuffed him with ideas of vengeance and establishing the truth and heaven knows what else — and now that he's done what you wanted him to do, you say you didn't mean it.'

'Not like this.'

'But how else could it have been? He's never been allowed to have a thought or a life of his own.'

'I don't understand.'

Mrs Marsh's head sank forward and the tears came freely. And it was all too clear that she didn't understand. This was not what she had wanted. She did not understand how things had got to this stage.

But Jessica understood. She had no proof that the final steps had been as she envisaged them, but she knew the men

311

concerned and knew how they would have acted. David must have approached Dampier and hinted that he knew something about Western's death. Dampier would have been only too ready to listen to anything about Western: greedy for facts or conjecture, wanting always to be omniscient, he would have walked happily into the trap. It was his job, his whole nature, to be perpetually inquisitive. They must have arranged to meet somewhere; David could have picked him up in the car, and then they had gone to a quiet place and David had demanded information on how best to get into Belby and find what he was looking for.

Dampier would have refused to talk. He must have been very stubborn. It had taken a considerable amount of torture to make him talk — the use of acid and a knife.

Jessica thought of herself in David's arms, and a wave of sickness came over her. She choked it back.

Dampier had talked. But he must have talked too late. David had gone too far. She told herself that he hadn't meant to kill Dampier, that he didn't know what he was doing, couldn't control his actions, wasn't really responsible for his actions . . .

This bowed, snivelling woman in the cellar was the responsible one.

Jessica said: 'But why did he keep . . . ' She couldn't say it. She could only nod towards the terrible crumpled heap in the corner. 'Why carry it round in the car?'

Mrs Marsh looked up suddenly. Her misery was transformed into a naive pleasure. 'Oh,' she said confidently, 'he wouldn't have wanted to leave it just anywhere. Once this was over, David would have wanted the poor man to have a decent burial. I'm sure that's what it was.' She nodded and smiled. 'David's a good boy,' she said. 'He's always been a good boy.'

'He's a liar,' said Jessica, 'and a murderer.'

'Never. I've never known him lie. How dare you say that?'

'He lied to me,' she recalled. 'I asked him if he had killed Philip Western.'

'I don't know who you're talking about.

Whoever it is, if David said he didn't do anything, then he didn't do anything. David,' said Mrs Marsh proudly, 'has been brought up to tell the truth. He always tells the exact truth.'

The exact truth ... Yes, thought Jessica, perhaps that was so. She had asked him specifically if he had pushed Philip Western over the rail in order to provide a vengeful parallel with what had happened to Mr Marsh, and he had said no. David the truthful, the meticulous, the believer in a truth that was always clear and sharp-edged and exact, would have felt quite justified in answering no if there had in fact been a slightly different motive for his murdering Western.

She wondered what his answer would have been if she had asked the plain, unadorned question — asked him simply if he had killed Philip Western. He might have come right out and said yes; or would he in his lucid but fanatical mind have found an excuse for telling a lie in order to reach what he considered a greater truth in the end?

'I don't understand,' Mrs Marsh wailed

again. It was a defensive cry. She was consolidating her refusal to understand so that eventually she would be able to assure herself that she was free from blame.

There was a faint sound from outside that could have been a car drawing up. There was a pause, then a dull thumping from the back of the house.

Jessica went to the foot of the cellar steps. She looked round for a weapon. The dismal light struck a muted reflection from the head of a hammer. Jessica went towards the bench. Mrs Marsh got there first. She grabbed the hammer.

'Oh, no, you don't!'

Faint footsteps paced overhead. Mrs Marsh held the hammer awkwardly like a croquet mallet and kept her gaze fixed on Jessica.

The footsteps went away and a muffled voice shouted something unintelligible. Then they returned and there was the sound of the key rattling in the lock at the top of the steps.

The door opened. A policeman came halfway down and saw Jessica. Over his shoulder he said: 'Looks as though she's all right sir. You can come on down.' Then he saw Mrs Marsh, and his eyes widened. 'Now, wait a minute . . . '

Mrs Marsh's fingers opened and the hammer clattered to the stone floor.

Andrew came hurrying down the steps behind the policeman.

Jessica said: 'Andrew! How did you . . . however did you know . . . ?'

'That's what personnel files are for, isn't it?' he said loudly, coming up to her and putting his arm round her. 'Home addresses and everything.' He tightened his grip. 'It's all right, Jess. It's all right.'

The policeman looked at the heap in the corner. 'What's this?' he said doubtfully.

He went closer; and saw what it was.

'My God,' said Andrew. He was holding Jessica as though wanting her, expecting her, to swoon against his shoulder; but he was the one who was trembling now. 'Oh, my God,' he said as the policeman carefully turned the body over and the light fell on what had been Dampier's face.

Poor Andrew, said Jessica to herself. She was grateful to him for coming, but it was an impersonal gratitude. Dear Andrew — she tried the words over and they meant nothing. She felt oddly detached. Poor Andrew. Poor David.

She was too numb to think, to feel, to respond.

13

There was a great soul-searching and a great exchange of mutual recriminations inside Intersyn. Someone must be at fault but it was hard to decide who. Public Relations Department worked feverishly in order to keep up a steady broadcast of 'No comment' in answer to all questions from the outside world. The Directors read the newspaper headlines, winced, and blamed Press Department for not finding some way of keeping the whole thing out of the papers. Memoranda choked the interdepartmental communication trolleys.

The dead men came in for rather more obloquy than sympathy. It was not done to get murdered. It was quite against Company policy. All these years there must have been some weakness in Western and Dampier that nobody had detected.

And as for young Marsh . . . it was

obvious that the entire system of personnel training and selection would have to be overhauled. Somewhere a terrible error had been made. Marsh ought never to have got as far as he did. He had been declared unfit to plead; he ought long ago to have been declared unfit to work for the Company. The causes of this misjudgment must be analysed. There would have to be meetings. Committees would be formed, reports written, a psychologist consulted; departmental heads would be asked to assess all their staff, and new slips of paper would be attached to the personnel files; several thousand pounds would be spent on printing a new handbook dealing with revised job grading methods.

By the time they had finished, the original reason for all this activity would have been happily forgotten. The activity would have become self-justifying and self-reproducing.

Anyone on a future Executive Course who mentioned Western, Dampier or Marsh would finish the Course with a large black mark against his name. He would never become good management material.

Andrew Flint's initiative in starting the final brainstorm session was noted by Partridge. So was Andrew's insistence on Partridge himself answering leading questions. Andrew got a good report from the Course, but not quite good enough. He was marked for promotion in a limited field.

If the Course could be said to have a winner, that winner was Hornbrook. He had comported himself admirably throughout. He had been resolute but not pushing. He was confident but not aggressive. He had quarrelled with nobody but was capable of showing firmness when it was necessary. Hornbrook was an ideal Intersyn type.

Andrew went home to Muriel, who said: 'Oh, you're back — do you get a prize, or have you been expelled?' And they had a drink and went out to dinner, and bickered in the car on the way home, and Andrew made love to her that night; and the next day he telephoned Jessica.

Jessica thanked him for his call and said

that she didn't really want to see him again. Andrew was irritated, then remembered how glad he had felt that it was all over and knew that his chivalrous gallop to her rescue had altered nothing. He was glad he had been the one to release her from that cellar. Somehow it rounded things off nice and neatly. He had drawn a line; he could start again.

There was a friend of Muriel's, a young woman separated from her husband, who had several times looked intently at him at parties. Once or twice she had held his hand longer than she need have done, and nowadays she expected him to kiss her cheek when they met or parted. He knew that she was waiting for him to kiss her on the lips. Then it would all start. It was risky, with her living so close to them and Muriel knowing her so well, but he knew that the time was right and that soon it would start.

Jessica gave in her notice to Intersyn.

She had planned a savage farewell speech. There were so many things she could say. But in the end they had a little party at which she was presented with a travelling clock, and there were drinks and jokes and everyone was sorry that she was leaving, so she just thanked them all and there was no speech, no parting fling.

She slept soundly that night and woke up feeling empty but gay.

THE END

We do hope that you have enjoyed reading this large print book.

Did you know that all of our titles are available for purchase?

We publish a wide range of high quality large print books including:
Romances, Mysteries, Classics
General Fiction
Non Fiction and Westerns

Special interest titles available in large print are:
The Little Oxford Dictionary
Music Book, Song Book
Hymn Book, Service Book

Also available from us courtesy of Oxford University Press:
Young Readers' Dictionary
(large print edition)
Young Readers' Thesaurus
(large print edition)

For further information or a free brochure, please contact us at:
Ulverscroft Large Print Books Ltd.,
The Green, Bradgate Road, Anstey,
Leicester, LE7 7FU, England.
Tel: (00 44) **0116 236 4325**
Fax: (00 44) **0116 234 0205**

THE COPPER BULLET

John Russell Fearn

Dr. Bland retires to his office to rest, complaining of a headache. But later, his fellow scientists find him slumped over his desk — dead. In his forehead is a round hole, edged with burn marks. He has apparently shot him-self — but there is no sign of a gun. The only clue is a copper bullet, of the type used in a .38 revolver. There is no cartridge cover — indicating that the bullet *has* been fired, and then put there . . .

THE UNIVERSAL HOLMES

Richard A. Lupoff

Sherlock Holmes is probably the most popular figure in world literature. For more than a century his adventures have been chronicled in books, on the stage and radio, in motion pictures and television. These Sherlock Holmes adventures show Conan Doyle's detective not only in his earliest days, but also in connection with the works of other authors — Edgar Allan Poe, Edgar Rice Burroughs, H. P. Lovecraft — as Holmes proves himself to be truly *The Universal Holmes*.

TOMORROW

E. C. Tubb

Seemingly with inside help, three men break into the laboratories of Atomic Power Inc., killing three guards and stealing a new formula for the control of atomic fission. However, the intruders are caught on camera, and one of them bears the dark streak of an indelible brand across his forehead — the debtor's mark! Private investigator Jim Carter knows that mark well, but in accepting the case to share the reward money with his informant — he's already marked for death . . .

THE CASES OF CHASE AND DELACROIX

Richard A. Lupoff

In the Great Depression, millionaire polymath Abel Chase and his associate, Claire Delacroix, are requested to investigate the San Francisco Police Department's most baffling cases: an actor found dead in his locked dressing room, with two tiny punctures in his neck; a deep-water explorer who disappears from his diving suit, sixty feet beneath the surface of Monterey Bay; and a test pilot who, on a flight with her passenger in an experimental fighter plane, emerges from cloud cover — alone!

THE ANGEL

Gerald Verner

For months, Scotland Yard was interested in the mysterious Angela Kesson, who they dubbed 'the Angel', with her striking beauty. Her male acquaintances had dubious reputations. And in every instance, at the start of each relationship, their homes were burgled and money and valuables stolen. Though unemployed, she lived in an expensive flat, but there was insufficient proof for an arrest. However when her latest escort's home was burgled — he had been murdered, his head crushed like an eggshell . . .